BRENTANO'S 1322 F STREET, N. W.

MINOR MIRACLE

ALSO BY AL MORGAN

NOVELS:

THE GREAT MAN
CAST OF CHARACTERS
ONE STAR GENERAL
A SMALL SUCCESS

SCREENPLAYS:

THE GREAT MAN—*with José Ferrer*
JALOPY—*with José Ferrer*

PLAYS:

OH CAPTAIN!—*with José Ferrer*

MINOR MIRACLE

AL MORGAN

DODD, MEAD & COMPANY - NEW YORK
1961

Copyright © 1961 by Albert E. Morgan
All rights reserved
No part of this book may be reproduced in any form
without permission in writing from the publisher

The characters, places, incidents and situations
in this book are imaginary and have no relation
to any person, place or actual happening

Library of Congress Catalog Card Number: 61-12317
Printed in the United States of America
by Vail-Ballou Press, Inc., Binghamton, N.Y.

FOR MARTHA . . . of course

CONTENTS

MINOR MIRACLE

FATHER Maurice Britt and St. Martin's Roman Catholic Church had a great deal in common. Both had grown old and gray in the service of the Faith.

St. Martin's had been built in 1907 in a style of architecture Father Britt once described as "Civil War Armory." When its doors were thrown open to its parishioners, it had dwarfed the brownstones around it and its spire could be seen eight blocks away.

In the years since, the church seemed to shrink as the buildings around it changed with the neighborhood. Today, St. Martin's is squeezed firmly between two thirty-story apartment houses, its spire unseen to anyone who is not standing directly in front of the church looking up to see it.

Between 1907 and the present, the neighborhood went through four distinct changes. The brownstones were the symbol of middle-class respectability, occupied mainly by the families of men with offices further downtown. Eleven o'clock was the signal (rung out by the bells of St. Martin's)

1

for a general exodus of nursemaids, babies and carriages, all bound for the greenery of Central Park. Around the fringes of this middle-class respectability were the tenements of the avenues, housing the German immigrants. Before the first world war, the parish of St. Martin's boasted more hofbraus and beer halls than Munich. In the twenties, the area changed drastically. The brownstones became rooming houses. The Germans in the tenements were joined by the Italians and the Czechs. During the depression years the brownstones went through still another change. They were gutted and made over into one-and-a-half-room units. The brownstones disappeared, one by one, in the forties, replaced by twenty- and thirty-story apartment houses, with their doormen, their elevator operators, their delivery entrances in the rear and their Tudor lobbies with black and white tiled floors. The neighborhood immediately surrounding St. Martin's became prosperous again but the avenues became more and more run-down. The tenements, unpainted for twenty years, seemed to settle into the dirt and squalor. Children living in the side-street apartment houses were forbidden to walk on the avenue alone. The tenement children amused themselves throwing dead cats at the apartment house doormen, terrorizing and robbing those apartment house children brave or foolish enough, lured by the penny candy of the stationery store on the corner to venture into the forbidden territory of the avenues.

The dichotomy of the neighborhood was apparent in the collection basket of St. Martin's, the pennies nestling side by side with the dollar bills of the apartment house dwellers. There were periodic complaints from parishioners

2

about the dirt that settled in the bottom of the holy water fount. Sermons were delivered mentioning that "Cleanliness is next to Godliness"; the sexton was assigned to clean out the fount twice a day and scrub the bottom of the basin but the dirt continued to settle. The combination of piety and cold-water tenements was immune to sermons and scrubbing. From its position as a wealthy, self-supporting church, in 1920, when Father Britt was assigned to the parish, St. Martin's had become, in the cold, hard words of the ledgers of the diocese of New York, a "moderately dependent church." In less formal words, that meant simply that it was not self-supporting and had become an object of charity of the Mother Church.

Father Maurice Britt, who had spent forty of his seventy-two years at St. Martin's, first as priest and then pastor, had aged along with the building—changing from an alert, aggressive young priest into an old man—becoming as much a part of the church as the tattered hymn books in the pews. He loved St. Martin's and had resisted all attempts to dislodge him for a better assignment. St. Martin's was his home.

He was equally at home sipping tea on a parish call in an adjoining apartment house or courageously downing a glass of home-brew in a tenement or a stein of bock in a *Turnverein* hall. He judged each of his parishioners on their worth as individuals and if he was prejudiced at all by the contrast between the apartment house and the tenement dwellers in his flock, he erred on the side of the well-heeled. He thought their road to heaven and a state of grace might be rockier and was not above attempting to widen the eye of the needle in their favor.

3

St. Martin's was a city church. Its playing fields were the sheep meadows of Central Park. Its annual yearly outing was a boat ride on the Hudson River Day Line to Bear Mountain. It sponsored bingo games one night a week, and raffled off, first, radios and then, TV sets. It earned a paragraph in "The Talk of the Town," in *The New Yorker,* as the first church in history to have neon halos over the statues of its saints. Father Britt had lost a close vote. After leading a futile fight against this final and, to him, most humiliating onslaught of modern civilization, he decided direct action was called for. Four successive accidents with the window pole destroyed four successive sets of neon halos and since that time, the saints of St. Martin's were haloless. "Halos," said Father Britt, "should be left to the eye of the beholder." "The Talk of the Town" took no further notice of the incident.

In his forty years at St. Martin's, Father Britt was officially reprimanded only twice. The first time was in 1926 when he organized a parochial baseball league and fielded a first-rate ball team, with himself in the pitcher's box. A certain amount of rivalry grew up between the churches in the league, but when the collection baskets began to mirror, on Sunday morning, the results of the ball teams' efforts on the ball field on Saturday, it came to the attention of the authorities. When it was discovered that rabid partisans of one church or another were betting a good portion of their weekly salary checks on their team the orders came to disband the league. Father Britt ventured the opinion that at least the money was not being spent in the local taverns and a healthy rivalry between parishes made for a healthier and livelier religious community. He was over-

4

ruled and since he had been hit on the index finger of his pitching hand the week before by a line drive and had no pitching replacement he bowed to the inevitable and disbanded his ball team.

The second time, gambling again brought him to the attention of his superiors. Noticing the drop in the receipts in the collection baskets week after week, he ran a lottery for three weeks. For a ten-cent service charge, a parishioner was permitted to write down his guess as to the amount of the collection the following Sunday. The closest guess would receive ten per cent of the collection. Father Britt felt that high-guessers would put more in the basket to boost the total, be rewarded for their zeal, and swell the church's coffers. The Bishop took a different attitude. He contended it was a horrible combination of communism and bookmaking. After this second incident, Father Britt found other, quieter outlets for his competitive gambling instincts and except for its inevitable yearly deficit, St. Martin's did nothing to bring itself to the attention of the Church hierarchy.

There was, quite realistically, nothing unique about St. Martin's.

In the body of a Church that runs the gamut from Notre Dame and St. Patrick's to a missionary's hut in Africa or Asia, St. Martin's must be described by anyone less fiercely partisan than Father Britt as a rather mediocre cog in a vast and complicated machine.

It suited Father Britt perfectly. He had never had any ambitions to rise in the inner councils of his chosen vocation. He had no desire to convert the heathen or play a part in the power politics of the Vatican. He was a parish priest.

5

The parishioners of St. Martin's were his people. That included the three who had been executed in Sing Sing during his forty years in the parish. It also included the five who were serving as priests in other parishes and the scattering of faithful who had gone on to careers in the state legislature, the law courts and, in at least one case, the pitcher's box at the Yankee Stadium. It included the wife-beaters, the Saturday-night drunks, the sneak thieves, the street cleaners, the taxi drivers, the subway motormen, the grocery clerks, the office boys, cleaning women, plumbers, steam fitters, laborers, and electricians, as well as the Tammany Sachem who always placed a brand-new, crisp, five-dollar bill in the collection basket at the eleven o'clock Mass on Sunday morning.

He was their friend as well as their confessor and spiritual leader.

In the rare moments of introspection, when he examined himself, his conscience, and his place in the Catholic Church, he came to the wry conclusion that his role was to play a sort of ecclesiastical drill sergeant in the Religious Basic Training Course. In his forty years at St. Martin's, he had had upward of thirty young priests serve as his assistants. All of them, sooner or later, began to doubt their call and their vocation. All of them looked to Father Britt as their conscience and their confessor. All of them, without exception, left St. Martin's reassured and ready for a useful, active life in the mainstream of Church activity. Father Britt, in quieting their doubts, quieted his own. In arguing their call and their vocation, he reaffirmed his own. He watched them arrive, waited for the inevitable confidences and saw them leave with pride, to be replaced by newer and more questioning seminary graduates.

Father Britt stayed on, saying his Masses, hearing his confessions, doling out his penances, teaching Church history to the Ladies' Sodality, calling the numbers at the bingo games, making sick calls, comforting the living and the dying, instructing the First Communion and Confirmation classes, marrying, burying, and advising—a parish priest.

SATURDAY

FATHER Britt finished his third cup of coffee of the morning, tucked a dime under the saucer and waved to the counter boy as he walked out of the coffee shop on the avenue. He leaned against the white porcelain front of the building, feeling on his face the hot sun of a June Saturday. He lit a cigarette and watched the Department of Sanitation men feed the contents of two huge garbage cans into the grinding machine at the rear of their truck. He wondered why he always timed his cup of coffee so that he came out just as the garbage trucks arrived. As he watched he felt the same irresistible impulse to jump into the grinding wheels that he used to feel standing on the platform of the subway watching an oncoming train rush toward him. He smiled.

Another first for St. Martin's, he thought. Priest commits suicide by jumping into garbage truck!

"What's so funny, Father?"

Willie Brandt came out of the tenement hallway and

8

joined him. Despite the calendar and the heat of the morning, Willie was wearing what Father Britt thought of as his uniform, a faded pair of Army olive-drab pants, an open brown vest and a heavy, dirty, woolen undershirt. He had a gray fedora on the back of his head and a toothpick in his mouth.

"Good morning, Willie."

"What's so funny, Father?"

"I was just wondering what it would be like to jump into that grinding machine."

"Damn uncomfortable."

"Do subway trains ever bother you, Willie, when you're standing on the platform?"

"How's that, Father?"

"Nothing, Willie. Just thinking out loud."

"I thought so," said Willie, scratching himself.

Father Britt took out his pack of cigarettes and extended it to the janitor. The janitor selected one carefully, tapped it against the back of his hand elegantly, put it in his mouth and leaned his head forward to allow Father Britt to light it for him. He exhaled the smoke luxuriously, scratched himself again and sat down contentedly on the empty ash can that had been replaced next to the stoop.

"I'll tell you the God's truth, Father," he said. "That's good."

How many mornings have I done this? Father Britt wondered. How many mornings have I had coffee in that lousy counter joint, come out, watched the garbage being chewed up mechanically and offered a cigarette to Willie? How many mornings has he selected it like a man choosing a diamond necklace for his wife? How many mornings

9

has he drawn that first drag, exhaled the smoke and said, "I'll tell you the God's truth, Father, that's good"? How many mornings?

"How many mornings have we done this, Willie?"

"I don't know, Father. Every morning since I've been here. Sixteen years. Every morning. Not counting Sundays. I guess you could figure it out."

"Sixteen years. Every morning. Not counting Sundays."

"That's right, Father."

"Sixteen years, wrestling garbage cans, cleaning the halls, listening to the complaints of the tenants. Don't you ever get sick of it, Willie?"

"I don't understand you, Father. Why should I get sick of it? It's what I do. It'd be like my asking you, don't you ever get sick of it. Begging your pardon, Father, like saying Mass . . . and listening to confession . . . and talking to the Ladies' Sodality and like that."

"Maybe I do, Willie."

"You're kidding, Father."

"Sure, Willie, I'm kidding. How are things going?"

"Can't complain, Father. Of course that damn Prosser kid is a cross. A cross, Father."

"What's he been up to now?"

"Writing dirty words on the walls again. Forgive me, Father, peeing behind the stairs. Things like that."

"I'll have a talk with him, Willie."

"I wish you would. I'll tell you, Father, don't talk too good to him. I'll tell you the truth, if he's going to heaven, I'm not sure I want to."

"You're kidding, Willie."

Willie looked at the priest. He colored. He scratched

10

his ribs. "I meant no harm, Father. It was just a joke . . . like that."

"I should hope so," said Father Britt. Now I'm baiting poor defenseless janitors, he thought.

"I mean . . . Father . . . It was just a joke."

"Willie, let me ask you something . . ."

"Sure, Father."

"How well do you know your catechism?"

"Well, I'll tell you, Father. I'm no book Catholic, you know? I mean . . . you know . . ."

"Does it say anywhere, Willie, that boredom's a sin?"

"How's that, Father?"

"Being bored. Wanting something to happen that hasn't happened every morning for sixteen years . . . or twenty years . . . or forty years . . . is that a sin, Willie?"

Willie looked puzzled. He stood still for a moment, thinking. "I don't think so, Father. I never thought about it much . . ."

"I just wondered. I can't find it listed anywhere as a sin."

Willie leaned closer. Father Britt reacted automatically. He stepped back from the honest smells of Willie's trade—dirt, sweat and garbage.

"Do you have anything good today, Father?"

"It's too early. Try me later, Willie."

"I'll do that, Father."

He put one of the large garbage cans on his shoulder and started up the front steps of the tenement.

"See you this afternoon, Father," he said, as he disappeared into the hallway with his burden.

Of course you will, thought Father Britt.

How many Saturdays have I listened to your confession? How many "evil thoughts of the flesh"? And where do you suppose he picked up that phrase? Evil thoughts of the flesh! A sixty-year-old man who smells sour, like the halls of the tenement he lives in, with evil thoughts of the flesh.

Someday for penance I'll suggest he take a cold shower. That way he'll get rid of the "evil thoughts of the flesh" and the sour smell simultaneously.

Father Britt continued down the street. He was stopped by two old ladies carrying shopping bags who told him at length about their pains and their aches and their novenas. He stopped again for a shoe shine. The Italian cobbler refused to accept the quarter he handed him.

"I'll take it out of my offering tomorrow, Father."

"I'm not sure God should have to pay for my shoe shines."

How many times have we both said exactly that? thought Father Britt. When does a joke cease to be a joke and become a ritual?

At the corner, he halted in front of a drugstore. The druggist was standing in front of the store window admiring a new display that featured a sexless, armless, legless and headless torso wearing a light tan truss. Father Britt came up behind him and slapped him on the shoulder. Without turning the druggist said, over his shoulder, "Hello, Maurie."

Herman Wekstein was probably the only resident of the area, Catholic or non-Catholic who did not call the priest "Father."

"Why should I call you that ridiculous name?" he'd asked. "You're not my father. Out of respect? Respect is

12

something that's gone out of the world. Even the doctors who come in here I call Doc. What should I call you—Pop? Better I call you Maurie. It will be a pleasant change. A man must get awfully sick of being called Father."

Father Britt looked admiringly at the display. One thing I'll say for it, he thought. It won't give Willie Brandt any evil thoughts of the flesh.

"Nobody has a rupture anymore," said Herman. "They all have hernias. You know what that is?"

"A truss."

"You'd think so, wouldn't you? It's like ruptures. There are no trusses anymore. That's an abdominal supporter. How's the cough?"

"Fine. That cough medicine worked fine, Herman."

"Good. It has a very high alcoholic content."

"Is that meant as an interracial slur?"

"I sell a lot of it. A lot of my customers tell me it's delicious on the rocks or with a little tonic water."

"I'll remember that."

"Come on in, Maurie. I was about to have some tea and a toasted bagel. Join me."

"It's against my religion."

"Maurie, did I ever tell you you're a very funny man?"

"Every morning for the past twelve years, Herman."

"Then it must be true. Anything that's repeated that often ceases to be just conversation. It takes on the dimensions of truth."

"I refuse to be drawn into one of your philosophical discussions this early in the morning."

"Sarah told me to invite you to dinner some night next week if I happened to run into you."

13

"If you happen to run into me?"

"I told her I might."

"The fact that you run into me every morning and have for the past twelve years didn't suggest to you that there was a strong possibility you would?"

"That's circumstantial evidence."

"And what night did Sarah suggest I come to dinner?" Herman laughed. Father Britt joined him.

"Wednesday," said Herman.

"How many Wednesdays have I had dinner with you in the past twelve years, Herman?"

"I think you missed two."

"Then you could have assumed I'd accept."

"That doesn't necessarily follow, Maurie. You might not."

"You could have taken it on faith."

"That's your business."

"And yours is spiked cough medicine."

"We're both in the business of giving the public what it seems to want. How about the bagel?"

"I just had coffee. Three cups."

"Who said anything about coffee?"

"I really can't, Herman. I have to get back to the rectory."

"You have your homework to do. After you stop off at the newsstand. Maurie, let me ask you something. How do you reconcile your homework and your Church's stand against gambling?"

"Who said the Church is opposed to gambling? Haven't you heard of bingo? There are more statues of more saints paid for by bingo than by pious parishioners."

"Can't they be both, pious and bingo players?"

"We like to think so."

"And you don't find it a contradiction that your Church calls gambling one of the major evils while you hustle bingo two nights a week and spend your morning handicapping eight races a day?"

"Except Sunday."

"Even the horses need a day of rest."

"Especially the horses."

"You don't find it contradictory?"

"Handicapping the horses? It's a hobby. It's a pastime. I never bet on them, Herman."

"No, you don't. But half your parish drop in on Mrs. Doody to find out if the Father has a good thing going today at Belmont. I can always tell when you've had a good day picking them, Maurie. Linkroum's bar is loaded that night with pious parishioners who made a killing on one of Father Britt's horses."

"Man does not live by cough medicine alone, Herman."

"Maurie, honestly, how can an irreverent old man like you be so religious?"

"It isn't easy. You know, Herman, I think you have something. It seems to me the regularity of stew and cheap meat as opposed to steaks and chops on the rectory dinner table is directly traceable to the speed of one of my selections. Do you think Mrs. Doody is dipping into the household money to place wagers?"

"You ought to know. You hear her confession."

"No, I don't. She always makes it a point to go to the assistant pastor. She told me she'd be embarrassed being around me if she confessed to me. I'll bet she's doing that, Herman . . . betting on the horses with the household money."

"Maurie, you amaze me."

"Sure and I'm delighted to hear that my good friend . . ."

"Maurie, please. Why does every Irish priest over sixty feel he has to slip into an imitation of Barry Fitzgerald every once in a while?"

"It's our compensation for the fact that you've converted Elizabeth Taylor. Do you really think Mrs. Doody is doing that?"

"Maurie, please. Sometimes you act like an infant. Ten minutes later I'm willing to swear you're a front for the Mafia."

"Herman! That's enough of that."

"Come on, Maurie. A joke."

"Sometimes a joke goes too far. It's a very unbecoming pastime, baiting a seventy-year-old priest."

"Seventy-two. But who's counting? You're not really mad, are you?"

"Of course I am. Herman, I don't care what you think about me in particular, or priests in general. I do demand some respect for the cloth. Of course I'm mad. Sometimes you go too far."

"Really, Maurie? Are you really?"

Father Britt smiled and tried to cover it by lighting a cigarette. "Not *very* mad, Herman."

"Tell me, Maurie. How did somebody like you get into this business?"

"Just lucky, I guess."

They both laughed.

"You kill me, Father Britt."

16

"No, I don't. But I may bury you."

"If there's anything I can't stand it's an aging Irishman with delusions of grandeur."

"You know, Herman, I think I'll have that bagel. It's always wise to keep an eye on the heathen."

Father Britt followed Herman Wekstein into the drugstore, past the racks of paperback books that he had, two years earlier, attacked from the pulpit; past the soda fountain, the aerosol cans of tooth paste, shaving soap and deodorants; past the showcase with its display of cameras and film; past the hairnets, candies, soap, hand lotions and toys. They walked through the archway that separated the smallest section of the store, the prescription cubicle, from the rest of the store. They passed on through to a small room in the back furnished with a stove, an oilcloth covered table, four chairs and a refrigerator.

How many years have I done this, Father Britt asked himself? How many mornings have Herman and I argued this way? How many times have I turned down the toasted bagel and wound up sitting at this table drinking tea out of a glass and eating the bagel, dripping with butter? And how is it that I feel more at home with this man than I do with any member of the parish? And what's the matter with me that I start making statistical records of everything I do this morning?

Herman poured the tea into the glasses, took the bagels from under the broiler, smeared butter on them and put them on plates and served them to himself and Father Britt. He sat in a chair across from him.

"Is anything wrong, Maurie?"

"No. Nothing."

"You seem disturbed this morning. Distant. No trouble with your chest lately?"

"None."

"Is that the truth?"

"Are you doubting the word of a priest?"

"Somebody has to."

"Herman. You know what it is? I'm bored."

"Everybody's bored. You've lived too long. That's one of the penalties."

"No jokes, Herman. I'm very serious. I'm so bored I could cry. I'm sick of everything happening the way it's always happened. Like before, when you asked me to dinner. You always ask me to dinner on Saturday morning and I always come on Wednesday night. Just once don't ask me. Or make it Tuesday."

"So come Tuesday. Don't make such a big thing out of it."

"Do you ever have a day when you start counting things? How many times you've put your socks on, how many cups of coffee you've had?"

"Everybody does."

"I suppose so."

"Don't forget, Maurie, you're in a very formal, repetitive line of work. Do you ever vary the Mass? Do you ever say anything different in the confession box? How many new sermons have you delivered in the past five years? You're repeating ones you did ten years ago. And ten years from now you'll be repeating ones you did fifteen years ago."

"Ten years from now . . . at seventy-two, you don't talk about ten years from now."

"You should worry. You have it made. If you're in the

right business, that is . . ."

"You were talking about the horses before. Why I do it. You know why I do it? Every race is different. It adds a note of uncertainty to a life that has too much certainty in it. Sometimes it gives me a small feeling of triumph to be able to sit down with some information and figure out that one horse may run faster than five other horses."

"I thought maybe it was just an antidote for the priest's vow of celibacy."

"I'm too old to be baited on that one, Herman."

"Don't you ever put two dollars on the nose of one of your horses?"

"Never. Would you bet on a crossword puzzle or a chess game?"

"That's a false premise and you know it. So you don't bet money and that keeps it from being gambling. Why should you bet money? What would you do with it if you won? Betting money, for you, would be foolish. You wouldn't be risking anything. You would still have the food Mrs. Doody serves you and a place to sleep. The fact that you do it at all is what is important and revealing."

"Revealing? I suppose you think it's revealing that I like once in a while to put on a sports shirt with an open collar instead of a clerical collar . . . or wear a loud tie or know what it's like to be on the pitching mound at the Yankee Stadium with the bases loaded and the game up for grabs. That doesn't mean I'm thinking of sending the Bishop my resignation."

"You want something to happen, is that it?"

"Don't you?"

"You're in the wrong business. In a drugstore something always happens. A woman gets something in her eye, it's a crisis. A boy puts a pot on his head and his mother can't get it off. A splinter won't come out with a red-hot needle heated by a match. Somebody has a stomach-ache. A baby has colic. A girl has to change the color of her hair for a date. Something always happens in a drugstore. In a church, I can see, it would be different."

"You don't have anything on your shelf for boredom?"

"A bottle magnesia, Maurie. You'd be surprised how the world can change with a bottle magnesia taken at the right time."

"I suppose so. At seventy-two I shouldn't expect surprises."

"At a hundred and seventy-two you should expect surprises. You don't have to get them but you should expect. How is Father Kincaid?"

"Fine. One of these days he's going to learn to smoke that pipe and even that small source of amusement will be denied me. Thank you for the bagel and the tea. I suppose Sarah is going to the movies tonight?"

"Saturday night. Of course."

"Why don't you drop around to the rectory after dinner . . . after she goes?"

"Don't I always?"

"Yes. Don't you always?"

"See you tonight, Maurie."

Father Britt walked out of the back room, through the drugstore and out onto the street. He walked to the curb to the newsstand. The crippled gnome behind the counter handed him a copy of the *Racing Form* and the *Morning Telegraph.*

20

"Morning, Father," he said. "Got something good to-day?"

"The Catholic Religion—across the board."

"I don't get you, Father."

"You're looking fine."

"Feel fine, Father."

"Good."

"See you this afternoon, Father."

Of course you will, thought Father Britt.

Let's see. He's the one who slips over to Jersey once a a month to a burlesque show. What's a burlesque show worth? two Hail Marys and five Our Fathers?

Father Britt folded the newspapers and tucked them under his arm. The distinctive masthead of the *Morning Telegraph* proclaimed to the world of the Avenue that here was a man bound for a quiet corner with a pencil to contemplate the eternal mysteries of the five-horse parlay or the daily double. He didn't so much flaunt the papers as wear them like an article of clothing. He had long since dismissed the idea of screening them with a copy of the *Times*. That would have suggested, to himself if to no one else, that there was something clandestine and shameful about his purchases.

As he walked slowly back toward the rectory, he opened the *Telegraph* to the box containing the experts' consensus. He was pleased to notice that Melissa's Husband was running in the second race. The horse, which had never finished better than third, was a particular favorite of his. The horse was dropping down in class, a fact that impressed the handicappers enough for them to pick him a solid third choice in the race. A lot they know, thought Father Britt.

He'll take it all.

He made it back to the rectory without being stopped by any member of the parish. His absorption in the paper gave him immunity. Father Britt's parishioners would no more have interrupted his study of the *Racing Form* than they would have interrupted him at his prayers. They were all aware of his passion for the form sheets and it had been a source of parish controversy for years. One faction (strongly supported by those who had profited from his study over the years) contended that it came under the heading of a hobby. Another faction was equally vocal in denouncing it as an unseemly preoccupation for a member of the clergy. The uneasy peace between the two factions had been sealed by Mrs. Ashlund, the three-hundred-pound tyrant of the Ladies' Sodality who silenced Father Britt's critics with, "What harm does it do? Would you rather have a drinking priest?"

Most members of the parish wound up being proud of their priest's peculiar passion. He was generally conceded to be superior to the syndicated touts employed by the tabloids. The more pious members of the parish pointed to his success at doping the races as still further evidence of the wisdom and brilliance of, first, the Irish race in general and second, Catholic priests.

There was, therefore, no reason for Father Britt to hide the papers on his way back to the rectory. Had he been seen, at this time of the morning, on this particular corner, without the *Morning Telegraph* and the *Racing Form,* the people of the Avenue would have taken it as a sure sign of some terrible calamity. It was reassuring to watch him walk around the corner, his head down, mentally assessing the chances of Melissa's Husband versus Take It All.

Father Britt had bought his morning papers . . . all was right with the world of St. Martin's.

As Father Britt opened the door of the rectory, he sniffed the air. It was an infallible way of telling whether Father Kincaid had returned from his parish calls. Father Kincaid was never seen by man or beast of St. Martin's without his pipe clenched between his teeth. It was always going out on him and he was continually striking wooden kitchen matches on the seat of his trousers, lighting it and taking asthmatic drags on it. Father Britt contended that Father Kincaid slept with the pipe clutched in his teeth and had had a long evening's discussion with Herman Wekstein about whether or not Father Kincaid simply turned the bowl upside down and continued smoking the pipe in the shower. He had volunteered to find out but hadn't had the courage to follow through and play Peeping Tom on his assistant. He did know that the members of the parish called Father Kincaid "Double F." The double F, standing for "frightened fish," was an inspired description of the way Father Kincaid looked, sucking in the sides of his cheeks in his continual combat to keep his pipe lit.

The air, that Saturday morning was free of tobacco smoke.

"Mrs. Doody, I'm home," he shouted up the stairs. There was no answer, but the sound of a vacuum cleaner being shut off was evidence that he had been heard. Mrs. Doody came down the stairs.

"Father Kincaid is making the sick calls," she said.

"Good," said Father Britt. "Unless he runs out of tobacco we won't see him until lunch."

"Him running out of tobacco would be like St. Patrick's running out of holy water. Father, can't we do something about his blushing?"

"What was it you had in mind, Mrs. Doody?"

"It isn't decent, Father. He's been here two years and he still blushes when he says good-morning . . . or good-night. I swear to the Holy Mother . . . the other day I saw him stop and pat a dog on the head outside the church. He blushed."

"The dog?"

"Father Kincaid."

"You disappoint me, Mrs. Doody. Is that worth keeping me from my work? Father Kincaid blushed? That's like saying a cow gave milk . . ."

"He's a problem one."

"He'll be all right, Mrs. Doody. He'll be a good priest."

"He's a fine one to send on sick calls, Father. If, God forbid, I was sick, would I want somebody bending over me looking like he just got hit in the face with a tomato?"

"He's the perfect choice for parish visits," said Father Britt. "The perfect choice."

Father Britt really believed it. In his own case, with the best intentions in the world, he'd never managed to make all the visits required during any given day. He would find himself involved in a conversation, a meal or a glass of beer and forget the time. He averaged three visits a day. Father Kincaid covered ten or twelve in a morning without ever seeming to light for more than a few minutes. He honored the household with his presence, smiled, said two "Hail Marys," and left. It worked fine for everybody. The parishioners were glad to see him go. He made them uncomfortable. They were embarrassed by him, because he was so obviously embarrassed by them: in some cases by their house, in others by their smell, their hospitality or their illness. He looked on the parish visit as a kind of clergy penance. He hated doing it but when Father Britt assigned him to it, he smiled and accepted. It would never have occurred to him to refuse or disagree. Only once had he voiced any opposition to his pastor. It was the memorable case of the neon halos. Father Britt erupted when the parish overruled his objections. Father Kincaid was conciliatory.

"Next thing you know," said Father Britt, "they'll be wanting me to put up a billboard outside the church. 'Today . . . at all masses . . . *The Ten Commandments*. You've seen the picture . . . now hear the original. Pride! Lust! Sin! Sin! Sin! *The Ten Commandments!* Ten! Count them! Ten!' "

"Don't you think, Father Britt . . . ?"

"Neon halos! Holy Mother of God . . ."

"Father Britt, it seems to me . . ."

"Why don't they put an electric sign on the collection basket that lights up and says 'Thank you' like they have at the toll booths on bridges?"

"Forgive me, Father . . ."

For I have sinned, added Father Britt, to himself.

"Forgive me, Father," repeated Father Kincaid. "We in the church mustn't forget that we are part of the twentieth century. Tradition is fine but we have to march with the times. If we don't object to lighting our churches with electricity instead of candles, why should we object to making use . . . for reverent purposes . . . of one of the major advances in electrical lighting? Neon, I am

25

told . . ."

Father Britt got red in the face. Father Kincaid matched his color with a blush, bent his head, took out a wooden kitchen match, struck it on the seat of his pants, lit his pipe, sucked in his cheeks and drew huge drafts of tobacco into his lungs.

"Father Kincaid . . ."

"Yes, Father Britt?"

"Why . . . don't you . . . go . . . say the Stations of the Cross . . . before they replace them with popcorn machines?"

It was the first and only disagreement the young priest and the old priest had.

Father Britt started toward his study.

"Mrs. Prosser is here with Rickie," said Mrs. Doody.

Father Britt stopped.

"Again?"

"Again," said Mrs. Doody.

"What's he done this time?"

"Same thing. I told her I didn't know whether you'd be able to see them this morning."

Father Britt almost accepted his housekeeper's unspoken offer.

"I told her," said Mrs. Doody, "you were out and you'd be busy when you got back."

"And what did she say to that?"

"She was rude."

"How rude, Mrs. Doody?"

"Just . . . rude, Father."

"What did she say?"

"Nothing, Father. Just the kind of rudeness you might

26

expect from the likes of her."

"Mrs. Doody!"

"She said it would do you good to get your head out of the scratch sheets and pay some attention to the young people in your parish. Begging your pardon, Father."

"She may be right, Mrs. Doody."

"Couldn't you leave it to him? He'll be back from his sick calls any minute."

"No. I don't think it's fair to Father Kincaid to expose him to Rickie Prosser. Or his mother."

"Especially his mother."

"Dirty words again, Mrs. Doody?"

"Yes, Father."

"Any special ones?"

"No, Father. Just the usual, I think. Willie Brandt caught him writing them on the walls of the hallway."

"Willie mentioned it to me."

"How he could read the dirty words on those dirty walls is beyond me."

"Where did you put them?"

"In the parlor."

"All right. I'll go in and see them. You can do something for me, Mrs. Doody."

"Anything you want, Father."

"While I'm with them, I'd appreciate it if you'd go through my files and pull out the last three races by Melissa's Husband."

"Is that one running again? Saints protect us!"

"Can do, Mrs. Doody. Can go all the way. Can take it all."

"That's easy for you to say, Father. It's just like a game

to you. You're not putting the two dollars on his nose."

"Nor are you, Mrs. Doody. Or are you?"

"Of course not, Father."

"I didn't think so. Maybe you'd better make it the last four races."

"All right, Father."

Mrs. Doody went into Father Britt's study. Father Britt put the newspapers on the hall table, reasoning that the less Mrs. Prosser saw of the *Racing Form* the less cause she would give him to be ashamed of his lack of charity toward a holy and pious woman.

When he entered the parlor, Mrs. Prosser was standing at the round table with a firm grip on the upper arm of her eleven-year-old son. She had evidently held the grip for quite a while because the boy's upper arm had turned white. When the priest entered the room she released her hold and turned toward him. The boy sauntered over to the sofa and sat down. Even from a distance of ten feet, Father Britt could see the whitened outline of her five fingers on the boy's arm.

"Rickie," she screamed, "stand up when Father Britt comes into the room. Who said you could sit down?"

"It's all right, Mrs. Prosser," said Father Britt. "Let the boy sit."

"I'll do nothing of the sort. If he can't show respect to his parents, he can at least show some to his priest. Stand up!"

Rickie stood up, wiped his nose with the back of his hand and stared at her with resigned patience.

"Hello, Rickie," said Father Britt.

"Hello, Father."

28

"You shouldn't even be talking to him, Father," said Mrs. Prosser. "A man of God like you shouldn't even be talking to a dirty-minded boy like that."

"Oh, he isn't that bad."

"Oh, isn't he? Ask him to tell you what he wrote on the walls at Willie Brandt's."

"The same words he wrote on the sides of the newsstand last week? The same ones he wrote on the school wall the week before?"

"The same, Father," said the boy.

"I don't know where he picks it up, Father. He certainly doesn't get it at home. I don't even know what half the words he writes mean. And Mr. Prosser certainly doesn't. Not only that, Father, he's been fighting. And playing hooky from school."

"Is that true, Rickie?"

"Yes, Father."

"And not only that, Father," continued Mrs. Prosser. "The other day I found him pitching pennies. Gambling, Father. The Lord only knows where he got the pennies from."

"Where did you get the pennies, Rickie?"

"I delivered some orders for Mr. Wekstein, Father."

"That's what he says. Wekstein! Fat lot that kind would give you! I don't know what to do, Father. The boy has me at my wit's end. Mr. Prosser says we should just put him in a home or the Protectory."

"Now, just a minute, Mrs. Prosser," said the priest. "Isn't that a little severe?"

"Severe? That's easy for you to say, Father. Gambling, I told you. Gambling! The next thing you know he'll be buying the *Racing Form* . . ."

Score one for you, Mrs. Prosser, thought Father Britt.

"What is it you want me to do, Mrs. Prosser?"

"You're the priest, Father. Talk to him. I can tell you, he's breaking his poor father's heart. I don't know what to do with him."

"Ma . . . I'm not . . ."

Mrs. Prosser bounded across the room, and seized the boy by the arm and shook him.

"Don't you talk back to me," she said as she slapped him across the face with her open hand. The boy started to cry.

"Ma . . . please, Ma. Please."

"You see, Father. Disobedient and rude. A rude, dirty-minded, disobedient boy. Don't you answer me back," she said, shaking him and slapping him again.

Father Britt walked over to her and grasped her arm. "Perhaps you ought to leave us alone for a few minutes, Mrs. Prosser. Why don't you go out in the kitchen and ask Mrs. Doody to give you a nice cup of tea."

"I'll do that," she said, giving the boy one more shake for good measure and releasing him with apparent reluctance. "I'll do that, Father. See that you give him a good talking to."

In spite of himself, Father Britt stepped aside as Mrs. Prosser walked past him. For a moment he had the frightening feeling that she might just grab him by his upper forearm and give him a good shaking too. When they were alone, the boy looked uncomfortably at the priest. Father Britt cleared his throat and prepared to give Rickie a good talking to. It was going to be difficult. He was fond of the

30

boy and had been since he had him in a first communion class four years before.

"Well, Rickie?"

"I know, Father. You're going to give me hell."

"I don't have to give it to you, Rickie. It seems to me you're earning it all by yourself."

The boy laughed.

"This is nothing to laugh about, Rickie."

"I know, Father. But you shouldn't say funny things. You always make me laugh."

"Why did you write the words on the walls?"

"I don't know, Father."

"You knew it wasn't right."

"Yes, Father."

"Good. Now what about the hooky?"

"I only played hooky four times. Four times all this year. Once to see the play-off game. Once for the seventh game of the Series. And twice to play baseball with St. Joseph's."

"St. Joseph's?"

"Yes, Father."

"You played on St. Joseph's baseball team?"

"We don't have a baseball team, Father."

"What about the pitching pennies?"

"I'm good at it."

"But it's gambling, Rickie."

"I know, Father. Honest, that isn't what's important. It's something I'm good at. They wouldn't let me do it if I didn't gamble. Honest, Father, I'd do it for nothing. Just for fun. If I could find anybody would do it just for fun. I practice a lot and I'm good at it."

"It's a hobby?"

"Yeah, Father. A hobby."

"I see. You know that gambling is wrong, Rickie?"

"Oh, sure, Father. It's not gambling, Father. Really it isn't. It's like you with the horses. That's not gambling. It's what you said, a hobby. With the pitching pennies, I don't care if I win or not. I just like to do it because I'm good at it."

"What position do you play on the St. Joseph team, Rickie?"

"I don't play with them regular. They just use me when they're short a man. I find out when somebody's sick and I show up. I play the outfield, Father."

The priest grabbed the boy's arm, gently. The boy automatically pulled back, grinned, and then stood still.

"You have a good arm, Rickie. Have you ever thought of pitching?"

"They won't let me pitch, Father. The big guys pitch. I'm lucky they let me play the outfield."

"Got a good arm out there?"

"Sure, Father. I threw two guys out at the plate in the last game."

"Two of them? Threw them out at the plate?"

"That's right, Father. I got a good arm. Everybody says so."

"Maybe some afternoon we'll go over to the park and you can throw some to me. After school, of course."

"Of course, Father."

"You've got the build of a pitcher, Rickie. Let's do that soon. I'll teach you how to throw a curve."

"Great, Father."

32

"It might be about time for St. Martin's to have a baseball team again. We could certainly use a good pitcher."

"Gee, Father, I'd like that. I mean, sometimes I feel like a traitor playing for St. Joseph's. It's not like they're Protestants or something but it ain't my parish, you know?"

"I know, Rickie. Now, what are we going to do about those dirty words on the walls, and playing hooky and pitching pennies?"

"Gosh, I don't know, Father . . ."

"You coming to confession this afternoon, Rickie?"

"Sure, Father."

"Good, Rickie. You just think about them between now and then. And Rickie . . ."

"Yes, Father?"

"Take the smile off your face when we go out of here. We wouldn't want your mother to think we enjoyed ourselves, would we?"

"No, Father."

By the time the priest and the boy emerged from the parlor they both looked properly subdued, serious and dour.

"I hope you gave him a good talking to," said Mrs. Prosser.

"I did indeed, Mrs. Prosser. Rickie's coming to confession this afternoon."

"I'll see that he gets there. I'll bring him myself."

"Fine."

"Thank you, Father," said Mrs. Prosser, extending her hand. "I hope we didn't keep you from anything important."

"No, nothing important," said Father Britt. "Just my usual morning exercise in equine logistics."

33

"Oh," said Mrs. Prosser, "that's nice."

"See you this afternoon, Rickie."

"You'll see him, Father. I'll make sure of that."

"I'm sure you will, Mrs. Prosser."

"Come on, you," said Mrs. Prosser, grabbing her son by the forearm again and yanking him along behind her.

Father Britt winced and almost asked her to treat a potential pitching arm with more care.

As Mrs. Prosser yanked Rickie along behind her through the hall she saw the two papers on the hall table. She paused, looked at them until she was certain that Father Britt had seen that she had seen them, snorted and walked out of the rectory.

Father Britt picked up the papers and went into his study. It was unlike any study in any rectory in any parish in any church in the Christian world.

The casual observer might have thought he was in the private office of the proprietor of a restaurant that specialized in a sporting clientele. Or the office of a pious bookie. The only religious articles in the room were a gaudily colored lithograph of the Sacred Heart in a 5 x 7 frame behind the closet door, and a crucifix. The rest of the wall space contained pictures of race horses, jockeys and race tracks. Two years before, Father Britt had requested a four-drawer steel filing cabinet to hold the records of the various church organizations. Two weeks after it arrived he decided it was a shame to waste the space with the meager collection of requisitions, minutes of meetings and attendance records. They were moved out and placed in a wooden grocery crate in the closet. The filing cabinet contained a complete file of the *Morning Telegraph* dating

34

back to 1955.

No member of St. Martin's parish had ever been inside the study. Father Britt was reasonably sure they would not understand the decorations and the purpose of the room. As a result, the rectory parlor was used for appointments and the general administrative tasks of the parish. It was abundantly decorated with religious pictures and objects.

Father Kincaid—Father Britt assumed—did not approve of the study, its decorations or of Father Britt's interest in the improvement of the breed. Not that he had ever said so. After seeing the study for the first time he was very careful not to cross its threshold again. If he had reason to talk to Father Britt while the older priest was closeted with his racing forms, he communicated with him through Mrs. Doody. If he had ever dared articulate his feelings about it, he'd have admitted to feeling as confused as if he'd discovered that his favorite aunt took opium in the sanctuary of her bedroom.

Herman Wekstein, on the other hand, was delighted with the room. Though he admitted that he didn't know a mare from a mudder he considered the room perfect for the kind of relaxed arguments and serious discussions that took place regularly between himself and the priest. He admitted to being confused by only one thing. He couldn't understand why Father Britt, who seemed obsessed by horses and horse racing, never went to a race track. In fact, Father Britt even refused to watch major races, like the Kentucky Derby or the Preakness on the rectory television set.

"They have nothing to do with each other," Father Britt told him. "The race track and the race itself have nothing to do with my hobby. I choose horses on logic, past performance, blood lines, track conditions, class, post position and jockey. The next morning I read what actually happened. I am right or I am wrong. I am not interested in the cheap thrill of actually watching them run. This way it is a puzzle and a stimulant to the intellect."

"Horsefeathers," said Herman. "You just don't dare watch them run. You'd get hooked. Not that you aren't hooked now."

Despite his flippant attitude toward criticism of his hobby, Father Britt searched his soul repeatedly. Was his preoccupation perhaps sinful? Was it becoming an obsession? Was it an unseemly occupation for a man of God? He frequently prayed for guidance. He sometimes went for two days without buying his morning papers, doping the races or looking at results, just to prove that he could quit any time he wanted to, just to prove that his immortal soul was not being threatened. He was proud of the fact that he did not buy back issues of the papers missed and that his file of the *Morning Telegraph* lacked eight or ten issues a year. He considered those missing issues his proof of nonaddiction. They proved that what he was doing was a harmless pastime and not an uncontrollable passion.

Mrs. Doody, who was sitting behind his desk with papers spread in front of her, rose when Father Britt entered the study.

"I'll tell you the truth, Father," she said. "I just don't see that horse. He's not dropping far enough down in class for that to matter. He shows nothing."

"We'll see," said Father Britt.

"Have they gone?"

"They've gone."

"Did you give him a good talking to?"

"Of course I did."

"Oh sure," said Mrs. Doody.

"I think the boy has the makings of a pitcher, Mrs. Doody."

"That just happened to come up while you were giving him a good talking to?"

Father Britt smiled.

"The mail came," said Mrs. Doody.

"Anything interesting?"

"A note from the Bishop."

"Did you check the last four outings?"

"The Bishop?"

"No. Melissa's Husband."

"Father, he has nothing. He's never been better than third. He ran seventh, ninth and sixth the last three times out."

"We'll see," said the priest. "Now get up from that desk and let me get to work. Is Father Kincaid back yet?"

"He's back."

"And?"

"And what, Father?"

"Everything go all right?"

"Why wouldn't it, Father?"

"Good. What's he doing now?"

"Reading his breviary."

"Good."

"I'll get out now and leave you to your work."

"Good."

Father Britt went to work. He put on his glasses, rolled up his sleeves, sharpened three pencils, spread the papers out on his large desk and concentrated on the first race.

He purposely avoided the second race, saving that, like dessert, for last. Mrs. Doody is right, he thought. Melissa's Husband really isn't much of a horse. It really doesn't have a chance, even dropping down in class. Why, he wondered, am I suddenly so interested in a lost cause? The attack of boredom that had hung on through the morning disappeared. He did not stop to think how many mornings he had spent at this desk doing the exact same thing with the racing papers spread in front of him.

He spent more time on the second race than he had on all the others and came to the reluctant conclusion that Producer's Folly, a solid seven to five choice on the morning line, was the obvious pick in the race. He checked its name and took the pad to write down his choices for Mrs. Doody. After writing "Second Race," on the pad he scrawled Melissa's Husband next to it and sighed.

God help me if it wins, he thought. I'll be sure it's divine revelation and I'll make something mysterious and mystical about even picking horses.

He went out to the kitchen where Mrs. Doody was preparing lunch and handed her the sheet of paper with his selections on them.

She glanced at the clock. "I was afraid you weren't going to make them in time," she said.

"Since when does that matter?"

"It's only twenty minutes until post time on the first race."

"Since we're not betting on them, Mrs. Doody, it really wouldn't matter if I didn't make the selections until suppertime would it?"

38

"No, Father," said Mrs. Doody hurriedly. "Of course not."

She glanced at the list. "You picked him," she said accusingly.

"He'll take it all," said Father Britt.

"I hope you're right, Father."

"It really doesn't matter, Mrs. Doody. It's just a sport, a game, a pastime. Isn't it?"

"Of course, Father. You really think he has a chance?"

"He'll take it all."

"That's good enough for me. Your lunch will be ready in a few minutes. Excuse me now, will you, Father? I must make a phone call."

"It wouldn't have anything to do with that list, would it?"

"Father, ask me no questions and I'll tell you no lies."

"You really do bet on them, don't you?"

"I'm not saying I do, mind. But suppose I did? Would it be the most terrible thing in the world? Would it be so terrible for an old woman to show some confidence in her priest?"

"There are worse things, I suppose."

"Father Kincaid will be wanting to talk to you, I'm sure, Father. He's in the parlor. Why don't you two have a nice chat and I'll have your lunch on the table in no time at all."

"Mrs. Doody, I swear to you, if I ever find out that you're betting on my selections, I'll stop doing it."

"You wouldn't do that, Father. You wouldn't, would you?"

"I would indeed. A game is one thing but gambling is something else."

"Gambling to excess, Father. That's a sin. You don't think an old woman like myself would do anything to excess now, do you?"

"Mrs. Doody, you sound like the Bishop on television."

"Sure and we all have our little vices, don't we, Father?"

"It's getting late, Mrs. Doody, and you wouldn't want to keep Father Kincaid waiting for his lunch, would you?"

"That I wouldn't, Father. Excuse me."

"Use the phone in the study," he shouted at her retreating back. "And don't count too heavily on Melissa's Husband."

"He'll take it all, Father," she said over her shoulder.

"He may at that," said Father Britt, to the empty room.

When he came into the parlor, Father Kincaid, who was sitting at the round table, writing, got to his feet.

"Sit down, Father Kincaid."

Father Kincaid blushed and reached for his pipe in the ash tray. He put it in his mouth, lit a match on the under surface of the table and took deep drags of tobacco.

"How did the parish calls go?" asked Father Britt.

"Very well. I made ten."

"About average."

"I'd have made more but Mrs. Ashlund insisted on giving me coffee."

"And how is Mrs. Ashlund?"

"All right. A little chest cold."

"Herman Wekstein has some wonderful cough medicine. Might be just the thing for Mrs. Ashlund."

"I'll get the name of it before I see her again."

"Yes. You do that, Father Kincaid."

40

"Forgive me, Father . . ." Father Kincaid paused.

Father Britt mentally completed the sentence again. For I have sinned.

"Yes, Father?" he said aloud.

"I was wondering if you'd prepared your sermon for tomorrow yet?"

"Not yet. I'll do it after confession."

Father Kincaid picked up the piece of paper he'd been writing on and got up, blushed and handed it to Father Britt.

"Forgive me, Father . . . but I thought you might have some use for this. It was just an idea I had."

Father Britt took the paper. It was headed: "The Mass Communications of Faith." After reading it, Father Britt handed it back to the young priest without saying anything.

"It was just a suggestion, Father," said Father Kincaid. "It seemed to me it had some valid ideas."

"Yes, Father Kincaid, I read it."

Father Kincaid blushed. It was a blush unlike the others. The others were normal, run-of-the-Kincaid blushes that were almost reflex actions. This blush was the Kincaid special. It was deeper and lasted longer and no amount of pipe smoking diminished it. It was reserved for special occasions. Usually after Father Kincaid was carried away by the sound of his own voice he blushed this special blush. After delivering a sermon he turned pink scarlet, and then deep maroon after he had finished and was safely back in the rectory.

"Forgive me, Father," he said, "I know you read it. I was just amplifying my point of view."

"I'll tell you what I'll do," said Father Britt. "It's a very deep thought and I wouldn't feel right using it. I think you should get full credit for it. Why don't you use it next time you have a sermon? We might even reprint it in the parish paper."

"That would be wonderful," said Father Kincaid.

"What do you think of Melissa's Husband, Father?"

"I'm afraid I don't know him."

"He can take it all, Father. And don't you forget it."

Father Kincaid was saved from commenting on this puzzling piece of information by the arrival of Mrs. Doody with the lunch tray. She set it down carefully on the round table, put two place mats on one side, sorted out the silver and placed a steaming plate of cabbage soup on each of the mats. The two priests pulled up chairs and started to eat their lunch.

Father Kincaid suddenly put down his spoon.

"We forgot something, Father," he said.

"Salt?" asked Father Britt. "Mrs. Doody," he shouted. "We forgot the salt."

Mrs. Doody poked her head into the parlor.

"It's right on the table. If it was a snake it would have bitten you."

"So it is," said Father Britt, reaching for the salt.

"That wasn't what I meant," said Father Kincaid.

"It wasn't?"

"No."

"Well, out with it. What did we forget?"

Father Kincaid blushed. "Grace," he said.

"Grace?"

"Grace."

It was Father Britt's turn to be embarrassed. It was the first time since he had been ordained that he had forgotten

42

the ritual of saying grace before a meal. Well, he thought, you wanted something out of the ordinary, didn't you? How about that? I forgot to say grace. Next thing you know I'll start stumbling over the Lord's Prayer or the Act of Contrition.

"Didn't you say grace, Father Kincaid?" he asked.

"No, Father."

"You didn't say grace to yourself before dipping into Mrs. Doody's cabbage soup?"

"No, Father."

"In that case, perhaps, we had better rectify that oversight."

The two priests bowed their heads.

"Will you say the grace, Father Kincaid?"

"Bless us, O Lord, for these Thy gifts and for what we are about to receive from Thy bountiful hands through Christ, our Lord, Amen."

"Amen," repeated Father Britt.

"I don't think that spoonful of unblessed cabbage soup is going to do you any harm," he said.

"No, Father."

"You know, there's a lot to be said for the Tibetan prayer wheel."

"You're joking, Father."

"Yes. I'm joking."

"I thought so."

"You were right."

The two priests ate in silence until the soup had been finished. Father Britt mopped up the last of the soup in the bottom of the bowl with a piece of bread and did not miss the slight grimace that suddenly passed across the face of

43

the younger priest.

I really do embarrass him, he thought. I'm afraid I'm not setting a very good example for the younger clergy. "Any complaints on your parish visits?" he asked.

"Mrs. Barrett complained again about the dirt in the bottom of the holy water fount. Her daughter has a boil."

"Where?"

Father Kincaid blushed.

"On her buttocks," he said.

"And?"

"And she claims she got the infection from the dirt in the holy water fount."

"Do you mean to say the youngster has been dunking her buttocks in the holy water fount?"

"No, Father."

"I should hope not."

"She claims the holy water fount is a disgrace and may be a source of infection to the whole parish."

"What did you tell her?"

"I told her we'd look into it."

"Of course. Anything else?"

"I met Mrs. Prosser on the street. Rickie has been writing obscenities on walls again."

"And playing hooky and fighting. They were in here. I gave the boy a talking to. He's coming to confession this afternoon. If you get him, Father Kincaid, be gentle with him."

"He *is* a problem, Father."

"He's eleven years old. That's his major problem."

"Yes, Father."

"If you should happen to get the mother, see if you can

44

find some support in the Scriptures for warning her about tampering with a God-given pitcher's arm."

"A pitcher's arm?"

"It's a sporting term, Father."

"Oh."

"Actually, I'm sure she'll come to *my* confession box. I'm sure she won't miss an opportunity to mention the horrible sin of gambling and sports forecasting."

Father Kincaid did not answer. He addressed himself to the sandwiches and tea. He was embarrassed that Father Britt had mentioned, even in such an oblique fashion what Father Kincaid could only think of as his "weakness."

As he ate, Father Britt looked occasionally at Father Kincaid. How young he is, he thought. How sure of himself. I wonder if he still blushes in the confession box. He remembered that almost five years must pass before the repetition of sins settled into a routine. It had been five years before, on any given Saturday, he could not be shocked by something a member of the parish had done, thought or contemplated. How long, he wondered, has it been since I've heard a new sin in the confessional?

Ate meat on Friday.

Used the Lord's name in vain.

Missed Mass.

Had evil thoughts of the flesh.

Abused myself.

Lied.

Cheated.

Stole.

Gossiped.

Committed adultery, fornication and blasphemy.

45

Read evil books.

Saw evil movies.

Went to the burlesque show.

Did not honor my father and mother.

Three times a parishioner had confessed to committing murder. The first time, just after he'd been ordained, he prayed for three days for guidance. But before he had to decide whether he could somehow serve justice and God without violating the oath of silence of the confessional, the murderer had confessed to the authorities. The other two men were apprehended by the law.

He had long since risen above the pleasures of listening to confession; had lost the faint worldly pleasure of sanctified eavesdropping. These people, whom he was human enough to like, dislike, or be indifferent to as individuals, became in the confessional part of an important and holy ritual in the relationship between priest and parishioner. When he slid open the wooden window separating the kneeling human being from the priest, and heard the murmured, "Bless Me, Father, for I have sinned," he became part of the mystery, beauty and mercy of his vocation. Each time he heard the murmured "Act of Contrition" with its rolling cadence, "Oh, my God, I am heartily sorry for having offended Thee," he was filled with a sense of wonder and confirmation.

Father Britt suspected that these emotions and that understanding were still ahead for Father Kincaid.

The priests finished their meal in silence and separated.

Father Kincaid went to his room to work on the details of the card party planned by the Ladies' Sodality that week. Father Britt went into the church and knelt at the altar rail. This hour of meditation, rosary beads in hand, was as inflexible a part of his daily routine as the morning walk to the newsstand. As he knelt this Saturday he asked forgiveness for the feelings of restlessness and boredom. He asked again for reassurance that his hobby, his form sheets, his handicapping of the races were nothing more than harmless diversions. He prayed for the sick and the well, the wise and the foolish, the wealthy and the poverty stricken, the arrogant, frightened, insecure and bitter. For an hour, he was a priest, on his knees in the presence of his God, asking for guidance, mercy and wisdom.

At three o'clock he conferred with the sexton and asked him again to see if something couldn't be done about keeping the holy water founts clean. He met with the choirmaster and helped select the hymns to be sung the next morning. He went to the study and answered his mail.

He wrote two letters of recommendation for youngsters of the parish who were applying for scholarships at Catholic colleges. He balanced the parish petty cash fund, sent a report to the Archdiocese and went over the menu for the Father and Son dinner with Mrs. Doody. He spent forty-five minutes with a young couple who were planning their wedding for the following month. He agreed with them that Bermuda was a wonderful place for a honeymoon and discouraged the bride from choosing Bach's "Come Sweet Death," instead of the more traditional Mendelssohn "Wedding March."

He checked through an estimate for repair and painting of the Rectory. Even to his casual eye, the figure seemed high. He scrawled a message across it, "Try a Catholic painter and contractor with a guilty conscience," and tossed the letter into the wooden file box on his desk.

Mrs. Doody came in and reminded him that it was a quarter to four.

"I don't suppose you'd be letting me put on the radio, would you, Father?"

"You just want to twist the dial a little?"

"And maybe have it come to rest on that station that gives the race results. What harm could it do, Father?"

"No, Mrs. Doody. No."

Mrs. Doody was asking him to violate one of his most cherished rules. He knew there was a radio station that broke into its rock-and-roll music all afternoon with racing results. He knew it had a large following in his parish. He refused to listen to it. Tuning in would give his handicapping too strident a note of commercialism. Hearing the results moved his hobby one notch closer to an obsession. However, it was his custom to send Mrs. Doody out at seven thirty to the corner newsstand when the early editions of the tabloids were delivered.

"I just thought, Father," she said, "that with him running in the second race you'd break your rule this once to find out what happened."

"He's just another horse, Mrs. Doody, and we won't be breaking any rules."

"Just as you say, Father."

It would have been very simple for Mrs. Doody to have slipped up to her room and listened to the radio on her bed-side table. She also could have called any one of a hundred friends on the phone and learned the race results. It would never have occurred to her to do either, without Father Britt's permission.

"Will you be going out tonight, Father?" she asked.

"Herman Wekstein is dropping in after dinner. Doesn't he always, Mrs. Doody?"

"Not always, Father."

"When did he miss?"

Mrs. Doody thought for a minute.

"I can't think right now, Father. But I know he did, once or twice."

"Well he won't tonight. Why?"

"Well . . . Father, if you weren't going to need me for anything I thought I might go to Loew's. They have a wonderful picture there with that darling Cary Grant."

"Did you check the Legion of Decency rating?"

"It got a B rating. Morally objectionable in part."

"And you'll just close your eyes and think of fields of yellow daisies in those parts?"

Mrs. Doody smiled. "Something like that, Father," she said.

The Legion of Decency had served Father Britt and Herman Wekstein as a rich source of discussion through many a Saturday night session. Father Britt had done his best to uphold the official Church position and defend the rating of motion pictures by the Legion. He would never have conceded to Herman that he thought the Legion and its dogmatic stands frequently ridiculous and almost always annoying. He remembered that many years before he had made a chart for himself of pictures in each of the Legion's categories. He had found many of the pictures that were listed as objectionable to be perfectly innocent and entertaining to anyone with any pretensions of being an adult. He had found several of the pictures given the A or approved ratings to be insulting to his intelligence and his Faith. Two biblical epics, which under the guise of religion had slashed lust, sex and unclothed females across the screen were particularly repellent to him despite the official blessing and praise of the Legion of Decency. He had refused, despite several pointed notes from superiors, to join in attacks from the pulpit against specific motion pictures and somehow never found room in the parish newspaper (a four-page mimeographed job) to print the Legion recommendations and condemnations. But Mrs. Doody carefully clipped the listing out of the *Catholic News* and pasted it on the mirror in her bedroom. Yet to the best of Father Britt's knowledge, the list had never kept her out of a movie theater.

"A B rating," said Father Britt, "should give you some pause, Mrs. Doody."

"It just means objectionable in part, Father. It's not like a C rating, is it? I mean . . . Father, really do you think Cary Grant could be objectionable in part?"

"There's something to be said for that," agreed the priest.

"Supper at six as usual?"

"Earlier if you want, Mrs. Doody. I wouldn't want to keep you from Cary Grant."

"I already checked the theater. The last show goes on at nine fifteen. You'll be doing your sermon after confession this afternoon?"

"Yes, Mrs. Doody."

"And what will it be this week, Father? Have you decided on anything yet?"

"I was thinking of preaching against horse-playing old ladies who flaunt the guidance of the Legion of Decency."

"Go on, Father. If that was the worst sin committed in

50

this parish, they'd have to be enlarging heaven."

"Is Father Kincaid ready?"

"He's waiting in the parlor."

Father Britt got up and walked out of the study, down the hall and into the parlor. Father Kincaid was sitting behind the desk reading his prayer book. He got to his feet, looked at his wrist watch, took one final drag on his pipe and emptied the bowl in the ash tray on the desk.

"Ready, Father?" he asked.

"Ready," said Father Britt.

The two priests walked out together and into the church. There were thirty or forty parishioners seated in the pews. Nobody was lined up at the confession boxes. Father Britt grinned. This was normal and unchanged too. He saw most of the heads turn surreptitiously in the pews to watch them as they approached the two confessionals that flanked the rear doors of the church.

Father Britt knew that they were watching carefully to see which priest entered which box. He knew that each had his favorite confessional priest just as each had his favorite movie star, shoe clerk or waitress in the diner. He knew that he had a reputation for being lenient and sometimes went out of his way to hand out a severe penance for a relatively minor collection of offenses just to keep his flock off-guard. God help the priest who doesn't stay one jump ahead of his parish, he thought.

"Any choice today?" he asked Father Kincaid.

"None. After you, Father."

Father Britt flipped a mental coin and walked into the door in the center of the confession box. He seated himself on the chair, adjusted the confessional stole, bowed his head, said the prayer he had been saying for forty-odd years before hearing confession and listened for the sounds from either side that told him penitents were kneeling in the darkness waiting for him to slide open the window and say, "Yes, my son."

Isn't it amazing, he thought, that in two thousand years nobody has managed to design something more pleasant, efficient or attractive for a confession box? In a parish where cleanliness ran a bad second to Godliness, the hours of confession became a test of physical endurance as well as priestly duty. Father Britt realized that he had completely forgotten to fortify himself with his usual confessional prop, a handkerchief dipped in after-shave lotion that was at least a small weapon against the smell of humanity.

I wonder who designed the first confession box, he thought. And why he rejected the idea of allowing as important and spiritual a relationship between man and God to take place in the open air where the participants could see the beauty of God's world around them as they recited their sins and were given absolution. And how did he ever think of anything as unpleasant as a priest sandwich? He smiled at that. I must remember to tell that definition to Herman. Or perhaps I'd better not. He has more than enough ammunition for his ridicule and scorn. But it is a priest sandwich, isn't it?

St. Martin's confessionals were built almost exactly like every other box in every other Catholic church in the world. Of course. The priest sat in the center, with partitions separating him from the kneeling suppliants on either side. The entrance to each of the side chambers was covered with a heavy red drapery that succeeded in keeping out the

52

air as well as the light. I suppose, he thought, there are good and valid reasons. We are all, to one degree or another, afraid of the dark and confession should be approached with some sense of foreboding. And after all, it is a sacrament and a mystery. Mysteries *should* happen in the dark.

He heard a cough to his right. He moved his head over toward the left side of the box and heard grunts that told him, as clearly as if he were watching, that a heavy person was settling down on the hard wooden kneeling rail next to the partition. Which side first?

I always start on the right. Fine.

The left. Something new. Something out of the ordinary. A small triumph for Father Britt against routine and the expected.

He slid open the wooden panel on the left side and could just make out the outline of a large feminine head.

"Yes, my daughter?" he asked.

"Forgive me, Father, for I have sinned . . ."

After the fifth confession, Father Britt found his mind wandering. He only half listened to the predictable chronicle of remembered transgressions. As a young priest he had felt guilty about his mind wandering in the confessional. He had prayed for guidance and had finally brought his problem to his pastor. "Of course your mind wandered," the pastor said. "It's supposed to. You don't suppose a priest could retain his sanity, week after week, listening to the same things over and over. He has human impatience. It is not a sin, my son. Only God has the divine patience to listen to confessions endlessly. The priest is not there as a man. He is there as a link between man and God. The confession is not being said to him. It is being said directly to

53

God. The priest is only a vehicle that transmits the confession to God. Let your mind wander. You'll know what kind of a penance to give. I find the confessional box a wonderful place to think about my sermons."

Father Britt did not prepare his sermons in the confessional but he did invent a series of competitions, again, simply as a means of keeping his mind on what he was doing. He knew, for instance, that he averaged twenty confessions an hour on a Saturday afternoon. He glanced at his watch frequently to see if he was proceeding on schedule. He was able to predict the five top-ranking sins on any given Saturday during any given season of the year. During the summer months the top three sins were always "missed Mass"; "evil thoughts or deeds"; and "ate meat on Friday." During the winter months it was "evil thoughts and deeds"; "disrespectful to my parents"; and "lying." It helped to know what your parishioners were up to in the sin department and, from the pulpit, it gave you an opportunity to hit them where it hurt the most.

He wondered about Father Kincaid's confession-box conduct. His assistant was probably just longing for a pipeful of tobacco. He did know that Father Kincaid was still delivering confession-box lectures, examining the sins as well as tallying them and as a result averaging a mere fifteen an hour.

Any day now he expected Father Kincaid to come to him, blush, and ask for guidance because his mind wandered during confession. Or did it?

"I ate meat on Friday, Father. I spoke disrespectfully to my parents. I used the name of the Lord in vain. I had evil thoughts about a girl in my class. I abused myself . . ."

"I hit my sister with a hard ball, on purpose . . ."

"I cheated on a test at school."

"I ate meat on Friday."

"I missed Mass . . ."

At five o'clock, Father Britt pushed aside the red drapery covering the outer door of the confession box. There were lines on both sides. Though the hours of confession were fixed it was understood that the priest would remain until all who wished to participate had been heard. He calculated that there were enough people waiting to require close to another hour. He hoped it wouldn't run much longer. Mrs. Doody had a movie to see and he hated meals that were thrown on the table hurriedly to meet the inflexible time-table of Loew's.

At six o'clock, Father Britt opened the sliding panel on the right-hand side and heard Rickie Prosser say, "Forgive me, Father, for I have sinned." He recited the same list of sins he had in the rectory parlor earlier that day, adding a few his mother hadn't known about. After he had said his "Act of Contrition," and been given his penance, Father Britt gave him absolution and said, "Go in peace, my son."

Father Britt closed the panel and moved over to the left side of the box and opened that panel. There was nobody in the chamber. He opened the door and looked out. No one was waiting. As he looked, Mrs. Prosser came out of the left side of Father Kincaid's confessional. The old priest took off his stole and emerged from the box. He walked down the center aisle noticing a few parishioners in their pews saying their penance; four old women standing in the aisle, rosary beads in hand, making the Stations of the Cross; and two women kneeling in front of the glass-cupped candles in front of the statue of the Madonna. Father Britt walked down the aisle to the alter rail, genuflected and went out the side door that connected with the rectory.

Father Kincaid was already seated at the table in the dining room and Father Britt slid into his seat, bowed his head and said the grace. Mrs. Doody, with one eye on the clock began serving the meal.

As she served the lamb chops, the lithograph of the head of Christ, which hung on the wall between the windows behind Father Britt, fell to the floor. Father Britt picked it up. The glass was not broken, nor was the picture wire strung across its back. He replaced it on the carpet tack in the wall and resumed his seat and applied himself to the meal. A few minutes later the door of the rectory burst open and Mrs. Prosser, propelling in front of her a crying Rickie, stormed into the room. The boy stood, with his head down, crying and sniveling.

"I'm sorry to intrude on you, Fathers," said Mrs. Prosser. "But something must be done about this boy. Stop your crying," she said, shaking Rickie and grabbing him by the arm.

Father Kincaid and Father Britt got to their feet.

"Mrs. Prosser," said Father Britt, "isn't it something that can wait a few minutes? Father Kincaid and I are having dinner. If you and Rickie will just wait in the parlor I'll be with you in a few minutes."

"It won't wait, Father," she said. "It won't wait. In the name of God, it won't wait, Father."

"The emphasis isn't necessary, Mrs. Prosser. If it won't wait, we'll discuss it now. What is it?"

Neither the child nor his mother said anything.

56

"Well, Mrs. Prosser," said Father Britt, "you said it wouldn't wait. What is it?"

Mrs. Prosser pushed the boy forward. His head was still down. He was still crying.

"Tell him," she said. "Tell Father Britt, the horrible, sinful thing you said. Tell him the blasphemy that crossed your lips in the church. And right after coming from confession. Tell him!" she shouted.

The boy looked up . . . looked at his mother first, then shifted his gaze to Father Kincaid, and finally his eyes came to rest on Father Britt. When he spoke he spoke quietly, almost in a whisper.

"I seen the Lady!"

Nobody moved or said anything for a few seconds. Father Britt crossed to the boy and put his arm around his shoulder.

"Tell me about it, Rickie," he said quietly.

"I seen the Lady, Father. Honest to God, I seen the Lady. Would I lie to you?"

"No, I don't think you would, Rickie. At least I hope you wouldn't."

"I seen the Lady, Father. I seen Her."

"All right, Rickie, let's start at the beginning."

"After I came out of confession," said the boy, "I went into the pew to say my penance. When I finished I looked up to see if Ma was finished. She wasn't. She was sitting two rows down from me and her head was bowed. I knew she was still praying. So she wasn't finished with her penance. And then I saw her, Father. The Lady. She was standing on the high altar. She looked down at me and then she walked down toward me. She got to the altar rail and she smiled and then . . . you won't believe this, Father."

57

"Try me, Rickie."

"Honest to God, Father. She smiled . . . at the altar rail and she . . . she just disappeared . . ."

"Blasphemy!" screamed Mrs. Prosser. She reached for the boy, but Father Britt turned him around, temporarily shielding him.

"You think you saw something, Rickie . . ."

"I seen the Lady, Father. The Madonna. She was real as life. First on the top altar and then she walked down to the rail and she smiled and then she disappeared."

"Rickie, let me tell you something. Sometimes people think they see something when they really don't. Sometimes their eyes play tricks on them, or the lighting casts a shadow, or they come out of confession with . . ."

"I seen her, Father. I seen the Lady."

"Rickie, listen to me . . ."

"No," said the boy, pulling away. He had started crying again and he stood in the corner, looking at all of them with defiance. The tears ran down his face and he sobbed.

"I seen her, Father. I seen the Lady. You can't tell me I didn't. I seen the Lady."

Mrs. Prosser rushed forward and grabbed Rickie by the arm. She was shouting, and red in the face.

"Stop it," she said. "Stop it! You bad, bad boy. Lying to a priest like that. Saying those crazy things. Blaspheming. Stop it . . ."

She shook the boy and suddenly lashed out and hit him across the face. The force of the blow knocked the boy against the wall. A thin trickle of blood came out of the corner of his mouth. He screamed and cried and pushed past her. She grabbed him again and held him firmly with one hand and hit him across the face with the other.

58

"Liar!" she screamed. "Liar. Liar."

Father Britt tried to pull her hand away from the boy. He was unable to loosen her grasp so he grabbed the hand that was hitting the boy and immobilized it in mid-air.

"Look!" shouted Rickie, "look!" He pointed.

They looked.

He was pointing at the picture on the wall, the portrait of the head of Christ, which had fallen to the floor earlier.

Mrs. Prosser was the first to see what he was pointing at. She released the boy, crossed herself and threw herself on her knees.

"The eyes opened," she said. "The eyes opened . . ."

She began sobbing and mumbling. "Holy Mary, Mother of God, pray for us sinners now and at the hour of our death."

Father Britt walked over to the picture. The eyes looked as they had always looked, with one important difference. In the corners of both eyes were drops of moisture . . . drops of moisture that looked like tears. As he watched, joined now by Father Kincaid and Mrs. Doody, the moisture ran down the cheeks of the picture.

Father Britt knelt in front of the picture.

"Our Father which art in heaven, Hallowed be thy name . . ."

Father Kincaid and Mrs. Doody knelt beside him and joined in the prayer.

"Thy kingdom come. Thy will be done in earth, as it is in heaven . . ."

"I told you," said Rickie, the only one still on his feet. He looked at the kneeling figures and repeated, "I told you . . . I told you. I seen the Lady . . ."

SATURDAY NIGHT

MRS. Doody never got to see the Cary Grant picture at Loew's that Saturday evening. After leading Mrs. Prosser, Rickie, Father Kincaid and Mrs. Doody in prayer, Father Britt sent the boy and his mother home.

"Remember," he reminded them, "don't talk about what happened in the church or here in this room. This has to be discussed and a course of action decided on. This is very important, Mrs. Prosser. You are not to say anything to anybody until you hear from me."

"Does that include Mr. Prosser?"

"That includes Mr. Prosser," said the priest.

"I'd *have* to tell him, Father."

"You will not say anything to anyone until I tell you. Do you understand that, Mrs. Prosser?"

"Yes, Father."

"And that includes Mr. Prosser. Understand?"

"Yes, Father."

"Good. Now you and Rickie go on home as if nothing

happened. And Rickie . . ."

"Yes, Father?"

"You understand what I've been saying, don't you? You understand that you're not to say anything about what happened until I say it's all right?"

"Yes, Father. I won't say nothing. I did see the Lady, Father. That's the truth. You know that now, don't you?"

Father Britt patted the boy on the head. "You're a good boy, Rickie and one of these days, real soon, we're going over to Central Park and try out that pitching arm of yours."

"Great, Father. That'd be great."

"Good. Now you two go on home."

The Prossers lived on the Avenue, right around the corner from the church. When they walked into the railroad flat, George Prosser, who had put in a hard day as a steam fitter, was sitting in the rocking chair with his feet up, drinking a can of beer.

"Where the hell have you two been?" he asked. "Is it too much a man should have his wife and his supper waiting for him? Where the hell have you been?"

"Confession," said Mrs. Prosser.

"So what've you got to confess it should take you this long?"

"George," said Mrs. Prosser, "which paper is it that gives you money if you call them up with something they can use?"

"What are you talking about?"

"The *News* or the *Mirror?* Which one?"

"How should I know? Will you please make me something to eat?"

Mrs. Prosser went out to the kitchen and pulled out the copies of the *News* and *Mirror* she had used to line the

61

bottom of the garbage can. She scraped off some crusted tuna fish and spread the papers out on the floor. She got down on her knees and turned the pages. On page seven of one of them she found what she was looking for. A small box on the right-hand side of the page was headed: "News Tips."

"If you are an eyewitness to a news event," it said, "And are the first to call this paper with the news tip we will pay ten dollars if you call this number." The number of the paper was given and beneath it a black line of type said, "Be a News Tipster and Earn Money!"

Mrs. Prosser carried the paper with her into the parlor and sat in the chair next to the phone.

"What's with my supper?" asked Mr. Prosser.

"Rickie, go put the fire under the stew on the stove."

"Stew!" said Mr. Prosser.

"It's Saturday night," said Mrs. Prosser. "What do you want, lamb chops? Have you any idea how much lamb chops cost?"

"All right. All right. Stew is fine."

"Go on, Rickie," said Mrs. Prosser, "put the fire on under the stew. I'll be out in a minute."

Rickie went into the kitchen.

"What are you doing?" asked Mr. Prosser.

"Being a news tipster, that's what I'm doing. Earning money."

She consulted the paper and dialed a number. "You think it's easy running the house on the lousy money you bring in. You try it sometime . . ."

"Watch your tongue," said Mr. Prosser, taking another slug of beer, "you been to confession."

"It wouldn't do *you* any harm to go to confession, George

Prosser. You put your head inside a church and the whole thing would fall down. And watch where you're putting that beer can, you'll get rings around my brand-new . . . Hello? This is Mrs. Prosser. I got a news tip. Like it says in the paper, I was an eyewitness."

"To a news event, madam?"

"That's what I'm saying. An eyewitness."

"I'll connect you. Just a moment."

Mrs. Prosser looked at her husband, smiled and winked. "They're connecting me," she said.

"Big deal. Sarah Prosser, cub reporter. What the hell is this all about?"

"I was an eyewitness. It'll be in all the papers. And get your big feet down off . . ."

"City Desk, Weldon speaking."

"This is Mrs. Prosser. I was an eyewitness."

"Yes, Mrs. Prosser," said the bored voice at the other end of the phone. "Now just what was it you witnessed?"

"A miracle. That's what it was. A miracle."

"I see. Just what kind of a miracle was it, Mrs. Prosser? Could you describe it to me, please?"

"Well, it was in St. Martin's. My son had just come out of confession and he looked up and saw the Lady."

"Which lady was that, Mrs. Prosser?"

"*The* Lady. The Madonna. The Blessed Mother. The Virgin Mary."

"All of them?"

"They're all the same. Just one."

"I see," said the voice. "I'll tell you what, Mrs. Prosser. We're kind of busy right now. Why don't you call back later . . . say about ten o'clock. My relief will be on then and he'll have plenty of time to talk to you. Be sure and tell him about those four women."

"They're the same woman. You're not a Catholic, are you?"

"Mrs. Prosser, I'll level with you. I ain't even a good newspaperman. Now why don't you call back later like a good little Kook."

"A what?"

"Kook. That's a newspaper term for news tipster. About ten, Mrs. Prosser, and be sure and tell him all about it."

"That isn't all."

"I figured. O.K., Mrs. Prosser. Shoot!"

"Well . . . after he saw the Lady . . . my son Rickie . . . we went to see Father Britt and while we were there in the rectory . . . the picture on the wall . . . the one of Christ behind Father Britt's head . . ."

"A picture of Christ behind Father Britt's head? Is that what you said, Mrs. Prosser?"

"The eyes opened and closed and the picture started to cry."

"The . . . picture . . . started to cry . . ."

"Real tears."

"Sure. And then what, Mrs. Prosser?"

"What do you mean then what?"

"Then what happened? I mean is that all there is to it? Your kid saw the Virgin Mary and this picture opened and closed it's eyes and cried tears . . . real tears. Is that the whole thing?"

"Of course that's the whole thing."

"I'll tell you, Mrs. Prosser. That's a swinging story."

"It's the Gospel truth. You should call Father Britt at

64

St. Martin's. He can tell you all about it."

"You know something, Mrs. Prosser? I may do just that. Father Britt . . . St. Martin's. Now do something for *me,* will you?"

"Of course I will."

"Fine. Hang up, will you? Maybe your keeper wants to use the phone."

Mrs. Prosser hung up before she realized she'd been insulted. "Smart aleck bastard," she said.

"Rickie saw the Lady," shouted George Prosser. "And the picture opened and closed it's eyes and then cried real tears. What the hell've you been smoking, Sarah?"

"Now don't *you* start. Shut up and come on out and eat your stew."

After Mrs. Prosser and Rickie left, Father Britt went to the wall and started to take down the picture of Christ.

"Should you be doing that, Father?" asked Father Kincaid.

"Why not?"

"It's evidence."

"Evidence of what?"

"Of . . ."

"A miracle, Father Kincaid? Is that what you were going to say?"

Father Kincaid picked his pipe up off the table and lit it. Mrs. Doody crossed herself.

"Now let's be realistic," said Father Britt.

"Realistic, Father?" said Father Kincaid vehemently. "Realistic after what we've seen?" He blushed at his outburst

and then continued in a quieter tone. "Forgive me, Father. I got excited. I just meant that, perhaps we shouldn't disturb the picture until somebody has seen it."

"The Bishop, you mean?"

"I think he should be notified of what happened here."

"Perhaps he should, Father Kincaid. First of all I think we should discuss what happened here. Or what we think happened. Come here a minute. You too, Mrs. Doody."

Mrs. Doody and Father Kincaid joined Father Britt in front of the picture.

"Now, let's not jump to any conclusions. Or say anything we *think* may have happened. Let's, for the moment, stick to the facts. You will both notice that there are two lines down the face of the picture, starting at the corner of each eye where moisture has run down. You both see that? The glass is smudged at the bottom but except for those two lines there is no evidence of any moisture on the picture now. Right?"

Mrs. Doody and Father Kincaid nodded.

"Now, Mrs. Doody," said Father Britt, "where were you and what did you actually see? Actually see, Mrs. Doody!"

"Well, Father, I was standing at the door. From the the kitchen I heard the boy crying and I came in to see what was going on. When I got to the doorway, she was hitting him across the face and then you, Father Britt, took the boy away from her and was talking to him. Then she grabbed him again and hit him again and called him a liar and then the boy pointed at the picture. And then we all looked."

"And what did *you* see, Mrs. Doody?"

"I saw the tears."

66

"You saw drops of moisture. Where?"

"In the corner of each eye. The eyes opened and closed and the tears fell . . ."

"Now just a minute, Mrs. Doody. The eyes opened and closed?"

"Yes, Father."

"Did you see them open and close?"

"Mrs. Prosser said they did."

"But did you actually see them open and close?"

"No. I don't think so. They were already closed again when I saw the tears fall."

"You just assumed they had opened and closed because Mrs. Prosser said they did?"

"I don't understand you, Father."

"You did not actually see the eyes open and close, did you?"

"No . . . but . . . Mrs. Prosser said they did. I did see a kind of a movement when I looked up. At the corner of the eyes. Like they had just closed again."

"But you did not actually see them open or close?"

"No."

"Father Kincaid, what did you see?"

"Well . . . Father, you want to know what I think?"

"Father Kincaid, what you think, at this point, couldn't interest me less. I want to know what you saw. What you actually saw. Not what you think or what Mrs. Prosser said or what conclusions Mrs. Doody reached. What you *saw*. Is that clear?"

"Yes, Father. In that case . . . all I saw were the two drops of moisture in the corners of the eyes in the picture and then I saw them run down the face of the picture. But,

Father Britt, it was a miracle. You can't dismiss it like this!"

"Who said anything about dismissing it? A miracle? Maybe. An imaginative young boy comes out of the darkness of the confessional . . . sits in a pew with his head in his hands, probably with his fingers pressing into his eyes, looks up and sees, or thinks he sees, a vision. Father Kincaid, do you know how often there are incidents like this? Not counting the inmates of asylums or hysterical young girls, or overzealous Christians. Thousands. Are they all miracles? Are miracles that commonplace? You listen to me, both of you. Do you know the harm that can be done with careless retelling of this story? Miracles, Father Kincaid and Mrs. Doody, are too rare, too important, too holy to be trifled with. So far we have no evidence except the word of an eleven-year-old boy who is not noted for his devotion to the truth. Is that enough basis for deciding it's a miracle?"

"What about the picture, Father?" asked Mrs. Doody. She crossed herself as she turned her head to look at it.

"That's something else again. Part of the picture incident is fact. It is fact that drops of moisture gathered at the corners of the eyes. We saw it. All of us. There are traces of it still down the face of the picture. But as far as the eyes opening and closing, none of us saw *that* except Mrs. Prosser and I don't think we can accept her word as incontrovertible evidence. You both act as if I'm trying to cover this up. I'm not, believe me. I'm just asking all of us to wait and examine the facts."

"Forgive me, Father . . ." said Father Kincaid. "Isn't that a decision for the Bishop?"

"I was wondering when you were going to mention that."

"Well, isn't it?"

Father Kincaid stared at Father Britt. For a moment, neither of them flinched. Finally the younger priest looked away.

"Father Kincaid, you don't know Bishop O'Leary, do you?"

"I haven't had that honor yet, Father."

Father Britt smiled. "I have. Do you know what the Bishop hates above everything else . . . and, Father, I include the devil, Pontius Pilate and French movies . . . above everything else? He hates to be bothered. So far there is nothing in this incident to suggest that my bringing it to the Bishop's attention would be anything but a bother. You'll have to trust my judgment in this, Father."

"I'm not doubting your judgment, Father Britt," said the young priest. "But we did see something. All of us. We saw the picture cry!"

"We saw moisture on the face of a picture that has been sitting in direct sunlight for more than twelve years. We saw that. Moisture. You continue to describe that moisture as tears. I say moisture. I do not rule out your miracle, Father Kincaid. I do not say they were not tears. Like the rest of you I was emotionally overcome when it happened. Now, later, in the light of reason and skepticism . . ."

"Skepticism, Father?" interrupted Father Kincaid.

"Yes. Skepticism. All we know for sure right now, is that moisture appeared on the face of the picture. I don't know whether the high humidity, the sunlight on the print or the glass caused it or whether there is some other, more divine explanation. I am not going to go off half-cocked about this thing. The greatest service we can all do our Church and our religion is to adopt an attitude of watchful, open-minded skepticism. There are enough people ready to heap scorn and ridicule on the Catholic Church without feeding them ammunition by proclaiming a miracle, which turns out to be, on closer examination, only the simple phenomenon of a picture sweating on a hot day."

"Sweating?"

"All right, Father. Perspiring. Is that better?"

"What do *we* do, Father?"

"We go on about our business as if it hadn't ever happened. I'm going to call Herman Wekstein and get his opinion on it."

"Herman Wekstein, Father?"

"Yes. Herman Wekstein. Anything wrong in that?"

"But he's a . . ."

"A Jew, Father? Is that what you were about to say?"

"I meant nothing by it. Certainly you don't think I'm anti-Semitic?"

"I don't think anything of the sort, one way or the other. I just want to know what you meant when you pussyfooted around with 'but he's a . . .' "

"All I meant was, isn't this a time to close ranks? 'Put none but Americans on guard tonight . . .' That sort of thing."

"First of all, Father Kincaid, Herman Wekstein—Jew, Catholic, Protestant or Holy Roller—is one of the smartest men I know. I'd like his opinion. Do you know what a Devil's Advocate is?"

"Of course I do, Father."

"I didn't mean to insult you."

"Excuse me, Father," said Mrs. Doody. "I don't."

70

"When the Church is about to canonize somebody, Mrs. Doody, the Vatican appoints a Devil's Advocate. It is his job to investigate the life of the potential saint and argue against his canonization. The Church feels, in this way, that by opposing and searching for evil, the good will be more and more apparent, if it is there. Canonization is a holy and important thing. It is more than enough to have one in a century. Are miracles any cheaper? Father Kincaid? Mrs. Doody? And what are the dimensions of your miracle? The word of an eleven-year-old boy, his hysterical mother, and some moisture on a picture. I think we could really use a Devil's Advocate and I think Herman Wekstein would fit the bill just fine. Any objections?"

Mrs. Doody and Father Kincaid remained silent.

"Good," said Father Britt. "I'll go call Herman and ask him to come over here tonight. You want to do something, Father Kincaid? I'd suggest you go to Mrs. Prosser and impress upon her all over again how important it is to keep quiet about this whole thing. If necessary, you can tell her that you've been thinking over her confession and this is an added penance. In her case I can't think of a stricter penance for anything short of murder."

"I'll do that, Father. Could it wait a minute or two?"

"Why?"

Father Kincaid blushed. "I haven't had my coffee yet."

"Mrs. Doody," said Father Britt. "Coffee for Father Kincaid, if you please. I'm going to call Herman."

At that moment the phone rang. Mrs. Doody answered it.

"For you Father Britt," she said.

Father Britt took the call in the hall. Mrs. Doody went

out to the kitchen and returned with a pot of coffee, two cups, silverware, cream and sugar and placed them on the parlor table.

Father Britt returned from his phone call. "Pour me a cup, Father Kincaid, will you? A good strong cup, if you please."

"Bad news?"

"That call was from one of America's great newspapers. Mrs. Prosser has let the cat out of the bag, I'm afraid. For ten dollars and immortality in the center fold. The reporter who took the call thought she was insane, but checked with me because, as he put it, it's a slow news night."

"What did you tell him, Father?"

"Are you suggesting that I would tell him anything but the truth?"

"Of course not. How much of the truth?"

"Just what I've been telling all of you."

"And?"

"He's sending a reporter and a photographer. I think we have to call the Chancery."

The Chancery on Fiftieth Street was the nerve center of the Archdiocese. The Cardinal was out of town and of the eight auxiliary bishops, only Bishop William O'Leary could be reached. He listened impatiently to Father Britt's explanation of the incident.

"I wish, Father Britt, you'd picked any other night but a Saturday to pull this one on me. It's been a very rough day."

"Your Grace, I assure you that I had nothing to do with either the incident or its timing. I merely thought you should know about it."

"Yes, Father Britt. All right. Now give the whole thing

to me again. Slowly. This kid saw a vision. Take it from there . . ."

Father Britt went through the whole story again. Slowly.

"Fine," said the bishop. "I got it. Now this newspaper feller that called you, you told it to him just that way?"

"Just about, Your Grace."

"You neither confirmed nor denied that it was a vision? You didn't give him the idea that the Church was supporting this story?"

"No."

"Good. Now how did he hear about it in the first place, Father Britt?"

"The mother of the boy called the paper."

"Why would she do that?"

"For ten dollars."

"What's that, Father Britt?"

"For ten dollars, Your Grace. They pay ten dollars to anyone who is an eyewitness to an event. She called them for the ten dollars."

"Father, can't you control your parishioners any better than that?"

"I don't understand you, Your Grace."

"Now look. I don't want this thing to get out of hand, you understand me, Father Britt?"

"Yes, Your Grace."

"Now remember, the kid came to you with this ridiculous story about seeing something. The kid's a liar, is he?"

"He's eleven years old."

"What's that got to do with it?"

"I mean he's no more a liar than any other eleven-year old. No less, either."

73

"Fine. The kid's a liar. You don't have to say it just that way, Father Britt. He's imaginative. He tends to get carried away into exaggeration. You get that?"

"Yes, Your Grace."

"Fine. I wish I could get up there and take over. You caught me at a very awkward time. Otherwise, Father Britt, I'd be right there with you, handling it for you."

"I know you would, Your Grace."

"You'd better get that picture off the wall. Put it in a nice safe place. I suppose you mentioned the picture to the reporter?"

"Mrs. Prosser did."

"Of course she did."

"What'll I tell the reporter when he asks to see the picture?"

"Tell him . . . Father Britt, you're on the scene there. I'm not. Do I have to make all the decisions for you? Tell him it's Church property and you can't show it to him without the permission of your superiors. Me. Pass the buck along to me."

"Just as you say, Your Grace."

"And please, Father Britt, don't let this thing get blown up into something important."

"I'm not really sure it isn't something important."

"Father Britt! Don't push the panic button!"

"I beg your pardon, Your Grace. I didn't understand you."

"I'm telling you, Father, it isn't something important. It's just a lying kid and his hysterical mother."

"As you said, I'm on the scene here and you're not."

"Now watch that tone, Father Britt. I haven't forgotten about that sinful lottery of yours, or the betting on those

74

baseball games. I don't mind telling you that your future at St. Martin's may depend on how well you handle this unfortunate little incident. Do you understand me, Father?"

"I understand you very well, Your Grace. I always have."

"Good. Now the whole thing will turn out to be nothing. It's just a lying kid and his hysterical mother. Be sure that's what it remains."

"Your Grace, I think you'd better talk to Father Kincaid."

"I'm sorry, I just don't have time. Now be a good boy and take care of this whole thing all by yourself, will you?"

"Father Kincaid is a very young priest, Your Grace. He's very impressed with what has happened tonight. I'm sure he'll want to talk to the reporter and give his opinion on the events."

"I get you. Put him on."

Father Britt lowered the receiver. "Father Kincaid, could you come here a moment?"

Father Kincaid came out carrying his coffee cup.

"The bishop wants to speak to you."

"Me?" asked Father Kincaid. "The bishop wants to speak to *me?*"

"He certainly does," said Father Britt, putting the phone in his hand.

Father Kincaid cleared his throat, blushed, and then spoke into the phone. "Your Grace? I just wanted to say what a great pleasure it is to talk to you. I've been an admirer of yours for a long time. I plan to mention your television program in the next sermon Father Britt allows me to . . . Yes, sir. Yes, Your Grace."

Father Kincaid held the phone and listened. He swallowed. He blushed. He nodded his head and finally said, "Yes, Your

Grace. You can count on me, Your Grace. It's been a great pleasure." He put the phone down.

"What did he say?" asked Father Britt.

"He told me I talk too much."

The phone rang again. And continued ringing for the rest of the evening. Mrs. Prosser's phone call with her news tip was like taking a finger out of the dike. The press services called, two local television programs, the news directors of five local radio stations and a lady who lived next door to the Prossers. She had heard about the incident and wanted Father Britt to know about a similar vision she had had at seven fifteen every morning for twenty-two years.

Fortunately, Herman Wekstein arrived at seven forty-five, was briefed on the details and put in charge of the rectory. At five minutes of eight, Father Britt and Father Kincaid went into the church to hear the Saturday evening confessions, leaving Herman in command as official press secretary and spokesman for St. Martin's. By ten, when Father Kincaid and Father Britt returned to the rectory from the confessional, St. Martin's was like a besieged city. Reporters, photographers, and morbidly curious parishioners arrived in platoons. Herman confided to Father Britt that he had removed the picture and put it away for safekeeping in the filing cabinet in the study. The reporters made Father Britt retell the story four times and posed him with Father Kincaid sitting at the rectory dining-room table.

At ten thirty Mrs. Doody burst into the parlor. Father Britt was telling the story again with four microphones in front of his face and the rectory parlor lit by the floodlights of the news cameramen.

"Excuse me, Father," she said. "I have to see you privately

for a moment . . ."

"Can't it wait, Mrs. Doody?" he asked.

"No, Father, it can't."

"Excuse me," said Father Britt to the nine reporters, four microphones, three tape recorders and one camera.

He followed Mrs. Doody out into the hall. She looked back over her shoulder and went into Father Britt's study. She closed the door behind her and sat in the chair beside his desk.

"Sit down, Father," she said.

Father Britt sat behind the desk.

"All right, Mrs. Doody, what is it?"

"A miracle, Father. A real honest-to-Gawd miracle."

"Mrs. Doody, please. I thought we agreed not to talk like that."

"I'm sorry, Father. That's the only word for it. A miracle . . ."

"An imaginative boy, his hysterical mother, it's . . ."

"Who's talking about *that,* Father? I'm talking about *this.*"

She spread the early editions of the tabloids across the desk in front of him.

"There's nothing in the papers about it yet, is there?"

"Of course there is."

"About Rickie and the picture?"

"Oh, that. No, Father. Here. *This* is what I'm talking about."

Father Britt bent down and looked at the paper.

"Holy Mother of God," he said.

"That's what I said," said Mrs. Doody. "Melissa's Husband won. He paid $38.40. I tell you Father Britt, it's a miracle."

"And two in one day is just too many for an old irish priest who was complaining that nothing ever happened and he was bored."

"$38.40," said Mrs. Doody.

"Amen," said Father Britt.

"Amen."

SUNDAY

J UDGING by the coverage of the story in the Sunday newspapers, Saturday had indeed been a slow news day. The *Daily News* had a front-page picture of Rickie Prosser standing midway in the center aisle of St. Martin's, pointing toward the altar. An artist had improved on nature by painting in the figure of the Madonna floating in space just above the altar rail. The headline writers christened the story, "The Miracle Of The Weeping Christ" and "The Vision Of Our Lady." The centerfold picture was a Prosser family group. Mr. and Mrs. Prosser and Rickie were kneeling in front of a statue of the Virgin Mary on the Prosser kitchen table. A discerning reader might have noticed the out-of-focus silhouette of a beer can in the lower left-hand corner of the picture. The accompanying story made much of the fact that reporters were not permitted to see the picture of the weeping Christ. To the rewrite man who had pounded out the story from the details supplied by a leg man on the scene at St. Martin's, this confirmed the suspicion that there was a genuine miracle involved. It was hinted that Church authorities had hidden the picture until their investigation was completed. The story suggested that it was only a matter of time before confirmation of the divine origin of the tears would be forthcoming from Rome and St. Martin's would replace Lourdes as one of the major Catholic shrines of the world.

The *Daily Mirror,* last on the scene the night before, leaned heavily on the wire-service story which merely repeated the actual details of the story as told by Father Britt. To make up for this, the *Mirror* had dug into the files and plastered pages three and four with a rewrite on Lourdes and St. Bernadette and a biography of Mother Cabrini. It was pointed out that Mother Cabrini was a local girl, and had been honored by having a boulevard in the Bronx named after her. It tied these two stories into the St. Martin's story with a question at the bottom of the page that asked, in heavy black type, the rhetorical question: WILL THE CRYING CHRIST AID WORLD PEACE?

The *Journal-American* had a red-banner headline above the masthead: "The Day the Picture Cried . . . Page Three."

It was a highly personalized rewrite from the wire-service stories, and read like the work of a man who had been awakened at midnight and told to file a couple of thousand words in a hurry.

The New York *Times* put the story in a box on an inside page. It simply stated the facts and was sprinkled with the newspaper weasel words, "alleged," "presumed," and "according to observers on the scene." It jumped to no conclusions, ventured no opinions, reported the story simply as a news item.

The *Herald Tribune* gave it two columns in the lower right-hand corner of page one. There was a picture of Bishop O'Leary and a statement by him that Church authorities were investigating the incident and would issue a report as soon as that investigation was completed. It was an unfortunate accident of timing that John Crosby's column in the radio and TV magazine supplement was devoted to a witheringly witty attack on "religious hucksterism."

All the morning news broadcasts on radio and TV carried the story and the TV programs used the same picture of Rickie pointing (without the artist's conception of the vision) toward the altar. The producers of two religious programs canceled the shows that had been previously taped for airing that Sunday and substituted discussions of miracles in general and the St. Martin's story in particular. WPIX moved a mobile unit to the curb outside St. Patrick's Cathedral and interviewed early-morning worshipers about the picture of the weeping Christ. One well-dressed woman contended that there couldn't be much to the story. "Why would it happen at a church like St. Martin's?" she asked. "If it was a genuine miracle it would have happened here at St. Patrick's, wouldn't it?"

The phone in the rectory at St. Martin's began ringing at dawn and Father Kincaid was told to answer it and deal with any problems presented by callers. He was given strict instructions by Father Britt, who left to celebrate the seven and nine-fifteen Masses with some trepidation and misgivings. Father Britt, who hadn't had time to prepare his sermon as he had planned, between Saturday night dinner and evening confession, pulled an old one out of the file. He relieved

Father Kincaid to allow him to celebrate the eight and eleven o'clock Masses. The Hungarian refugee priest who turned up every Sunday to celebrate the 12:15 Mass (the Archdiocese continued to promise Father Britt an additional regular priest in place of the one who had been assigned elsewhere the year before) spoke no English at all and was of no use in the rectory. He left after serving at the Mass.

It was a busy morning for Father Britt and Father Kincaid as both of them tried to deal with members of the press who now considered the "miracle" a major news story.

Father Kincaid turned down an invitation for Father Britt to take a bow on the Ed Sullivan show that night. There were calls from the "Today" show and the Jack Paar show asking if Father Britt would like to be interviewed. There were calls from the Barry Gray show, Long John, and a young man at WBAI who asked permission to record the ten o'clock Mass providing Father Britt was officiating. David Susskind's office called and wondered if Father Britt was free to appear on "Open End" that night. The participants included two Algerian newspapermen, an English night-club comic and the editor of the *Realist*. The caller felt that Father Britt would fit into that group very well. When Father Kincaid declined, it was suggested that they might work out a solo appearance for Father Britt, providing he brought along the picture.

Father Kincaid enjoyed himself thoroughly. He felt that he had suddenly been lifted out of obscurity and put at the hub of the universe. He managed to tell each caller how much he personally enjoyed reading his column, watching his TV show, or listening to his broadcast. After the first three calls, when Father Kincaid had found his second verbal wind, he ended each conversation with, "May the blessing of God be upon you, my son."

The reporters and photographers began arriving shortly after ten o'clock and were severely reprimanded by the sexton for dropping their used flash bulbs in the holy water fount. They were also forbidden to take pictures inside the church while a Mass was in progress.

The church was only half filled for the seven o'clock Mass, normally unpopular and sparsely attended. By nine-fifteen the church was jammed with standees three deep in the rear. The whole neighborhood had seen the morning papers and put on their best clothes to go to church, pay homage to God and become part of a news event.

Sight-seers from other parts of the city began arriving for the eleven o'clock Mass and the local police precinct sent two extra patrolmen to the front of the church to direct traffic and keep the crowd on the sidewalks in motion. Hawkers sprang up, circulating through the crowd, selling post-card-size replicas of the lithograph that had hung in the rectory parlor. "Here y'are, authentic replicas of the Weeping Christ. Two bits. Authentic replicas. Get them while they last."

The crowd bought them, but somehow they seemed to last. The hawkers had an unlimited supply.

The high point of the excitement outside the church was reached shortly after noon when the entire Prosser family arrived for the twelve-fifteen Mass. Mrs. Prosser was wearing her corset (in honor of her new-found celebrity) and a flowered print dress bought a week before in the rummage shop for a dollar and a quarter. Rickie had his hair slicked down with greasy tonic, and Mr. Prosser was wearing his burying suit. He had worn it before only at his wedding, his induction into the Knights of Columbus and at the Steam Fitters Ball. The most striking part of his wardrobe was a large, red, hand-painted tie, featuring a nude lady with a toothy provocative smile. The wearing of the tie had been a source of considerable argument in the Prosser household as they were dressing for this public appearance. Mr. Prosser had remained firm. "It's the best tie I own," he said. "Cost me two bucks. You want me to look nice, don't you?"

Mrs. Prosser agreed, with reservations. "You open your jacket just once," she warned, "and I'll clobber you."

As they climbed the church steps, photographers knelt before them, asking for the inevitable "Just one more, please." The Prossers did not consider it an imposition or an invasion of privacy. They'd have been content to remain on the church steps, smiling, waving or looking serious all day long, or at least until the photographers' flash-bulb supply ran out.

Mrs. Doody fluttered around, enjoying the excitement and, in a rare combination of Christian charity and morbid curiosity, carried two huge picnic-type thermos jugs of coffee to the reporters on the sidewalk.

Herman Wekstein arrived shortly after noon. "You were bored," he said. "You wanted something to happen."

Father Britt smiled and motioned him into a chair beside him in the study. Herman manned the telephone and confused several callers by identifying himself as Herman Wekstein, assistant to Father Britt, pastor of St. Martin's.

Mrs. Doody carried the emptied coffee jugs into the kitchen and knocked at the door of Father Britt's study.

Then she opened the door and said, "May I come in, Father?"

"Come in, Mrs. Doody. You might be able to spell us on the phone for a while."

"I'd be delighted, Father," she said. "Isn't it exciting?" Father Britt grunted.

"Did you see the papers this morning, Father?" she asked.

"I certainly did," said Father Britt.

"The sports section?"

"I never got out of Lourdes."

"It really *was* almost a miracle, Father," said Mrs. Doody. "He was dead last coming into the stretch. And then it must have been like the hand of God had reached down and pushed him. He came on with a rush and won by three lengths. Three lengths, Father."

Herman Wekstein looked puzzled.

"Melissa's Husband," explained Father Britt. "An eighteen to one shot I picked in the second race yesterday. He won. Paid $38.40."

"Yesterday was your day, Maurie," said Wekstein. "Everybody is entitled to one day in his life when everything goes right. Yours was yesterday. You should have bought a sweepstake ticket, or tried swimming the Hudson, the long way . . . or pitching for the Yankees."

"$38.40," said Mrs. Doody as Herman reached for the ringing telephone.

"Tell me something, Mrs. Doody? Tell me the truth. No lying to me today. Did you bet on Melissa's Husband?"

"Yes, Father."

"How much, Mrs. Doody?"

"Only five dollars, Father."

"On the nose?"

"Of course. It doesn't pay to bet place or show. I mean, Father, I did it only as a mark of respect for my priest. I didn't dream of winning. What kind of respect would I be showing, betting it to place or show?"

"You must have won over ninety dollars, Mrs. Doody."

"Yes, Father."

"A good day's work."

"Oh, I intend putting half of it into the collection basket, Father."

"Of course you do," said Father Britt.

At one o'clock exactly, a long, black Cadillac pulled up at the door of the rectory. A chauffeur opened the back door and two men got out. They were a strange contrast. One, dressed in a black Italian silk suit and a stiff clergyman's collar, was an imposing figure of tremendous proportions.

At first glance, except for the clergyman's collar, he might have been mistaken for an all-American tackle or a heavy-weight contender. The second figure was just about half his size and height. This smaller man was wearing a seersucker suit, a clip-on bow tie, and carried a dispatch case. The two of them pushed their way through the knot of reporters and climbed the steps of the rectory.

"When do we get to see the picture, Bishop?" one of the reporters shouted.

"How about a statement, Bishop?"

"We've been here all morning. We have deadlines to worry about . . ."

The bishop halted at the door. "There will be a press conference in exactly thirty minutes," he said.

"Will we get to see the picture, Bishop?"

"I can't tell you that, yet."

"Does the Church have an official position on the vision, Bishop?"

"I'll be glad to answer your questions in thirty minutes. Now," said the bishop, "you'll just have to wait until I've talked to Father Britt. We'll be happy to answer all your questions in the rectory in thirty minutes."

"Will the boy and his mother be at the press conference, Bishop?"

The bishop smiled again and opened the rectory door and went in.

Mrs. Doody had been standing at the window when the Cadillac arrived. She had alerted Father Britt so when the bishop entered he was greeted in the front hall by the priest. They shook hands.

"This," said Bishop O'Leary, pointing to the short man in the seersucker suit, "is Biff Rogers. Biff, this is Father Britt."

"How are you, Father," said Rogers, extending his hand. "You've really been tearing up the pea patch, haven't you?"

Father Britt smiled tentatively and shook hands.

"Biff, here," said Bishop O'Leary, "is a friend of mine and public-relations man for one of the networks. I figured we could use a little expert advice the way things seem to be going. I suppose you couldn't do anything about preventing this thing from blowing up the way it has, could you, Father?"

"I don't think so, Your Grace."

"We'll talk about that later. First of all, you'd better send somebody to get that kid and his mother over here. I promised the reporters I'd hold a press conference in half an hour."

"I'll go, Your Grace," said Mrs. Doody, curtsying nervously.

"Fine," said the bishop. "Now let's go into your study where we won't be disturbed and talk this whole thing over. I want to put Biff in the picture firsthand."

"Let's go into the parlor," said Father Britt.

"Too public. Too accessible. We'll go into your study, Father."

"It's not very comfortable," said Father Britt. "I think you'd be much more comfortable in the parlor."

"I didn't come here for a vacation, Father. Your study!"

"Yes, Your Grace. Follow me."

Father Britt led the way with all the speed and pleasure of a man walking toward the door of the execution chamber It might as well be, he thought, when the bishop gets a look at the pictures on the wall.

"This is an interesting experience for me," said Biff Rogers. "I'm not a Catholic, you know. Oh, I have great respect for your faith, Bishop, and, you know, we're all playing in the same ballyard. I find it very interesting to have a backstage peek at the way the holy water splashes."

Bishop O'Leary laughed. "You certainly have a wonderfully colorful way of talking, Biff."

"Glad you like it, Bishop. I mean no disrespect by it. I may talk lightly about things like that but if you'll notice I'm standing retreat like the rest of you."

"What did he say?" asked Father Britt.

88

"Said he's standing retreat," whispered the bishop.

"What does it mean?" whispered Father Britt.

"Show-business talk," said the bishop. "Very colorful, don't you think?"

"Oh, yes," said Father Britt. "Well here we are. Are you sure you wouldn't rather go into the parlor?"

"This'll be fine."

Father Britt took a deep breath, opened the door and stepped aside to let the bishop and Biff Rogers enter first. Then he waited a moment for the explosion he knew would come when the bishop saw the pictures hanging on the walls. Hearing nothing, he entered the room himself. Herman Wekstein was standing in front of the desk, smiling. The walls were completely bare.

"I cleaned up a little, Father," said Herman.

"I see that. Your Grace, this is Herman Wekstein. Herman, Bishop O'Leary."

They shook hands and the bishop introduced Biff Rogers. They shook hands.

"Now," said the bishop, "if you'll pardon us, Mr. Wekstein, Father Britt and I have something rather serious to discuss."

"Herman is my public-relations adviser," said Father Britt. "Like Mr. Rogers is yours. He isn't a Catholic either."

The bishop frowned, seemed about to say something, looked at his watch and then nodded "All right," he said. "Father Britt, will you tell Biff the facts. Not your interpretations of them—just the facts."

Father Britt, who knew the story by heart went through it once again. When he finished, Rogers said, "Check."

"Bishop," he went on, "I think what you have to decide

right now, before the press conference, is whether you want to ride the raft or sink it." Noticing the puzzled expressions on the faces of Father Britt and Herman Wekstein, he explained.

"What I mean is, do you want this story to stay alive or do you want to just let it die? If you want it to stay alive you got a good gimmick in the picture. Don't let them see it. If you want it to die, just trot out all the props, give them both barrels and wait for something else to happen that will take you off the front pages."

"Well . . ." said the bishop, "I've consulted with some of the other authorities in the Diocese. Unfortunately, the Cardinal is away and the other Bishops are unavailable. They tell me that it is my problem."

"That's a plus, Bishop," said Biff Rogers. "You're the image. Some of it has to rub off on you."

Bishop O'Leary looked embarrassed. "Biff, I think you should understand that I am here today acting as an auxiliary bishop of the Archdiocese of New York. I am not interested in this from the standpoint of publicity . . . personal or otherwise. I have a duty in this instance that overrides any personal gain involved."

"Sure, Bishop," said Biff, "we all understand that. You're here as a bishop, right?"

O'Leary nodded and went on, "Now, let me tell you all the official position of the Catholic Church on incidents like this one. As I'm sure you know, things of this sort crop up all the time. Somebody gets overemotional and sees something. Or has indigestion and sees something. Or wants to see something so much that he succeeds. The Church's position is to oppose accepting any of these incidents as being miraculous until every other avenue of explanation has been exhausted. Until then the only possible explanation is that it is, in fact, miraculous. Anything else would be pure superstition. And this Church is not founded on superstition and needs no trickery or suspicion of trickery to survive. In short, our attitude must be one of skepticism."

Father Britt smiled.

"May I ask something, Bishop?" said Herman Wekstein.

"Of course."

"Suppose, for sake of argument, right at this moment you looked up and saw a vision, similar to the vision the boy claims to have seen in the church. What would your reaction be?"

"I would doubt the evidence of my senses. I am a realistic man, Mr. Wekstein, as well as a bishop of my Church. I believe in my Church, my God and my religion. I need no cheap reassurance."

"But suppose, Bishop," continued Herman, "suppose all of us in this room saw the same thing?"

"That wouldn't change it. I'm told the indian rope trick, perhaps the most famous piece of magic in the world, has been accomplished before crowds of people. The explanation, I'm told, is a case of mass hypnotism. With the events of the past twenty-four hours it would not be difficult for any of us to imagine we were seeing things we weren't seeing at all. In this particular case, Mr. Wekstein, I expect to exhaust every possible avenue of investigation before I even begin to admit the remote possibility of there being anything miraculous about the boy's vision or, as the newspapers call it, the Weeping Christ."

"Great word coinage," said Biff Rogers.

"In short, Mr. Wekstein," continued the bishop, "though I tell you quite simply that I am a deeply religious man, I strongly doubt the reality of any miracle."

"Your Grace," said Father Britt, "how many Masses do you suppose you've said in your lifetime?"

"I couldn't even guess, Father. Certainly thousands."

"And haven't you yourself been part of a miracle every time you've said Mass? Why will you accept one miracle without question and not even admit the possibility of another?"

"They have nothing in common, Father."

"Haven't they, Your Grace? I'm seventy-two years old and yet every time that miracle happens I am filled with wonder, elation and belief. What I'm saying, Your Grace, is that it is not as impossible for me to believe that there may be more to this incident, as you call it, than an eleven-year-old boy's exaggeration and the hysteria of his mother. We all saw the moisture on the picture. That much at least, Your Grace, is fact."

"I intend to investigate that."

"How?"

"I intend sending the picture to a laboratory to run a chemical analysis of the moisture. Let us find out what resemblance it bears to tears, scientifically."

There was a knock on the door. Father Britt called, "Come in" and Father Kincaid entered the room.

"I hope I'm not intruding," said Father Kincaid. "Mrs. Doody said you were in here and you'd probably want to see . . ."

He paused, and looked at the walls of the study.

"We've redecorated, Father. In honor of His Grace's

visit," said Father Britt.

"What's that?" asked the bishop.

Father Britt ignored the question and introduced Father Kincaid to the bishop. Father Kincaid kneeled and reached for the bishop's ring to kiss it.

Biff Rogers looked at his watch and walked over to Bishop O'Leary.

"It's close to a half hour, Bishop," Rogers reminded him. "What's the decision?"

The bishop looked around. "This thing has been blown up out of all proportion now," he said. "It seems to me the only thing to do is to give them everything we have. That includes the picture. I mean we'll show them the picture, let them interview to their heart's content, and continue our own investigation quietly. I would guess that the whole thing will be forgotten within five days. Would that be your guess, Rogers?"

"Sooner, Bishop, if any kind of news breaks."

"Fine. Father Britt, will you get the picture?"

"The Prossers are outside, Your Grace. I saw them sitting in the parlor with Mrs. Doody when I came in."

"Thank you, Father Kincaid," said the bishop.

"Father Britt, have you any idea where we can hold the press conference? From the looks of things on the street, they'll never fit in here, or the parlor for that matter."

"Excuse me, Father," said Father Kincaid. "What about the recreation room in the basement of the church?"

"That sounds fine," said the older priest. "Any objections, Your Grace?"

"None at all. Father Kincaid, why don't you go out and take charge of the press? Escort them into the recreation room. The rest of us will be along in a few minutes."

"Yes, Your Grace," said Father Kincaid. He almost skipped to the door.

"You might take Mrs. Prosser down, after the reporters are settled in. If there's an anteroom, keep the mother and boy in there until the rest of us arrive. I don't want the reporters turned loose on them without somebody around to control things."

"You can trust me, Your Grace," said Father Kincaid.

"I'm sure I can," said the bishop, smiling the smile that one advertising executive said was worth ten armored divisions in the battle against sin.

"How do you stand him, Father?" asked the bishop when Father Kincaid left.

"He's a fine young priest," said Father Britt.

"To eat meals with three times a day? Well . . . let's get organized. Where is the painting?"

"In the filing cabinet."

"Rogers, why don't you and Wekstein go on down to the recreation room and see if you can give Father Kincaid a hand."

"I get you, Bishop," said Rogers. "For 'give a hand' read 'keep your eye on.' "

"Come on, Father Britt, let's take a look at that famous Weeping Christ of yours."

"May I suggest something?" asked Herman.

The bishop nodded.

"You don't want to walk in with the picture in your hands, do you? That will stampede your press conference before you can get it organized. Will it fit in Mr. Rogers' brief case?"

94

"That's a dispatch case," corrected Biff Rogers. "Mark Cross."

"Will it fit in Mr. Rogers' dispatch case . . . Mark Cross?" repeated Herman.

"Father Britt?" asked the bishop.

"I'm sure it will. That's a good idea, Herman. We'll put the picture in it and bring it down to the press conference that way."

"Good thinking, Wekstein," said the bishop.

"Creative," added Rogers.

"In a drugstore," said Herman Wekstein, "there are always crises."

Fifteen minutes later, when Father Britt and Bishop O'Leary walked into the recreation hall, things were completely under control. Mrs. Doody had set up coffee urns and cups on a table in the rear and the thirty reporters and photographers were seated in front of the stage. When the priest and the bishop entered they got to their feet. Nobody was quite sure whether they acted this way out of respect or just to get a better look. In the case of the photographers there was no doubt. They climbed on top of chairs and snapped their pictures. Mrs. Prosser and Rickie followed, and George Prosser, with his coat jacket still buttoned, took a seat in the rear of the room.

Father Kincaid had arranged four chairs on the stage. The Prossers occupied two of them, Father Britt sat in a third and the fourth was for the bishop who showed no inclination to sit in it. He was obviously determined to chairman the meeting and face the questions on his feet. Biff Rogers and Herman Wekstein walked to the rear of the room and found seats next to George Prosser. Herman looked at the tie and winked. George Prosser grinned, saw that Mrs. Prosser was busy talking to Father Britt on the stage and flashed open his coat quickly to give Herman a quick glance at the wonders of the painted lady. Herman nodded his approval and was told the price of the tie.

"Gentlemen," said the bishop, "I'm going to level with you all the way this afternoon but I must insist on a few ground rules. First of all, I'll be happy to answer any questions about the incident. You may question any of the people on the platform with me—the boy, Mrs. Prosser, and Father Britt. Our intention is not to withhold any information. I must, however, ask that certain questions and certain answers be off the record. They are for your background information only and if they are used in the body of your story, they are not to be attributed to any of us."

"Why is that, Bishop?" asked a reporter in the first row.

"Because," said the bishop, turning on his smile, "there are things I can tell you as a man who understands your problem with a complex story and who wants to give you a quick course in the history of the Catholic Church and incidents of this sort. But I couldn't possibly tell you such things—wearing my other hat—as a bishop of the Archdiocese of New York. If you have any objections to those ground rules I'm afraid I can talk to you only as a bishop. I don't think, in the present instance, you would find that as satisfactory."

"Fair enough," said the reporter.

"Besides," added the bishop, "I wouldn't want you to get me into trouble with my boss. And I'm not talking about the sponsor of my television show.

"Now, you all know the facts of the situation we are

gathered here to discuss. If I were to judge it purely on the basis of what I read in the papers this morning or heard on the air or saw on television I would come to the conclusion that a genuine gold-plated miracle took place here yesterday afternoon. I don't happen to believe that. The Church doesn't happen to believe that—yet. We are investigating the occurrence and when that investigation is completed, we—and by we I mean the Catholic Archdiocese of New York—will issue a statement. Until then there will be no official announcement from anybody connected with the Church. Is that understood?" The bishop paused.

Father Kincaid came out on stage with a folded bridge table. He put it up and left to return with a pitcher of water and four glasses. The bishop poured himself a drink and continued.

"All right," said the bishop. "Now, if you'll pardon a little criticism from a man who sometimes pokes his ecclesiastical nose into your industry, I think you have overplayed this story outrageously. I won't attack you on the grounds of blasphemy because I don't know enough about your individual religious beliefs . . . if any . . ."

The bishop paused for his laugh and got it.

"I will, however, attack you on the grounds of good taste. Really, gentlemen . . . that picture on the front page of the *News* this morning was not only insulting and blasphemous but bad art work. I am here today, frankly, in the hope that we can approach this situation with a little more taste, judgment, and maturity and put it in its proper perspective. This, I repeat, is an incident. It is not yet a miracle. And it is certainly not a circus . . . and I must admit, gentlemen, when I drove up here this afternoon that's what it resembled. Now if you're ready, I am. If you will just raise your hand, I will recognize you. The gentleman in the back row."

"Bishop, you keep calling it an incident . . ."

"Because that's what it is."

"Would you mind giving us your personal opinion?"

"Off the record?" asked the bishop.

"If it must be."

"It must be. Let me take them one at a time. First the vision. I'm going to assume none of you in the audience are Catholics. That way I can explain it simply, so that you will all understand what I'm talking about. Confession, in our religion, is an important, holy and solemn part of the dogma. A Catholic in the confessional is talking, not to a priest but directly to God. To God, gentlemen. If you are a Catholic you believe that, and you are going to take it seriously . . . whether you are fifty years old, ninety years old or, in this case, eleven. When you have finished your confession and are given absolution by the priest, you come out of that confessional with a load lifted from your shoulders. The load of sin. You are in a state of grace. I know . . . psychologists would explain it away by telling you that the lifting of guilt by confession to *anyone* would give you the same lift. Perhaps so. I won't argue that. This is not a confirmation class or a mission. I am not trying to convert the members of the Newspaper Guild."

The bishop got another laugh and let it run its course before continuing.

"What I am saying is that yesterday afternoon this eleven-year-old boy came out of the confessional in a state of grace, knelt in a pew in the church and said his prayers to a God he had just spoken to directly. He raised his head and saw something. Or thought he saw something. We are, all of us, you, me, and this eleven-year-old boy, conditioned animals. We see what we expect to see a lot of the time. And yesterday afternoon that boy was conditioned to see something. It didn't surprise him that he did. I just won't accept, on his word alone—and I am not saying the boy was lying—I will not accept as fact what he says he saw—not without something to substantiate it. And so far there is nothing to substantiate it."

Rickie Prosser jumped to his feet.

"I seen the Lady," he said. "I did. I'm not lying. I seen the Lady."

Father Britt went to the boy and put an arm around his shoulder and sat him down.

"Now let me take the second part of the incident," continued the bishop, as though there had been no interruption.

"The picture. Gentlemen, have you ever seen the walls of your rooms perspire during a hot spell? Have you thought it was evidence of a miracle? It is evidence that summer is here, that plaster or wallpaper retains moisture and gives it off. That, I'm afraid, is the simple solution to the picture incident."

A hand was raised in the second row. The bishop acknowledged it.

"Bishop, you sound to me as though you've prejudged the case. You said there was an investigation. You sound as if that investigation is over before it started."

"I will not make the investigation by myself. I am only giving you my opinion of the incident. My effort is to give you one possible explanation for an incident that you all assume is miraculous. The Church, gentlemen, is an old institution. Again, off the record, I'll be willing to guarantee you that a great many events of the distant past which were accepted as true miracles would have been easily explained away in the light of our present sophistication and knowledge.

"Believe me gentlemen, if there *is* a miracle, it will be apparent that it *is* one and any investigation of a true miracle will only point up its divine origin. You accuse me of prejudging this situation. Perhaps I am. I am only telling you that on the surface and on the basis of my experience and knowledge it seems to me very unlikely that we are involved with anything supernatural."

A reporter midway in the auditorium asked a question of Mrs. Prosser. "Mrs. Prosser, you claimed that you saw the eyes of the picture open. Is that true?"

Mrs. Prosser got to her feet.

"I said it," she assured him.

"You heard the bishop just now? Do you still say you saw the eyes open and close?"

"I know what I seen," said Mrs. Prosser.

"Nobody else saw them."

"I don't care if the Pope himself said it. I know what I seen. I seen the eyes open and close."

"Any comment on that, Bishop?" asked the reporter.

"None at all," said the bishop.

"Good," said Biff Rogers to Herman Wekstein. "Very dangerous to contradict a woman on a platform. He's almost home free."

Another reporter was on his feet. "Bishop, you say you are starting an investigation . . ."

"I said an investigation was under way. I did not say I personally was conducting it."

"Are you, or aren't, you?"

"I can't answer that question."

"All right," said the reporter, "what would the investigation consist of?"

"I would assume that the boy and his mother would be questioned again, at length. I assume that the picture would be sent to a laboratory to get a chemical analysis of the moisture. Beyond that I can't give you any further details."

"How about the picture, Bishop? Do we get to see it?"

"Of course you do. Father Britt, would you show the picture, please?"

The photographers climbed up on their seats again. Some of them rushed forward to the foot of the stage and stood, cameras poised, as Father Britt got to his feet and opened the dispatch case.

He took out the picture and held it up.

Flash bulbs popped and all the reporters came down to the foot of the stage for a closer look. The photographers continued to snap their pictures.

"Bishop," said one photographer, "would you mind pointing toward the picture?"

"I'll do nothing of the sort," said the bishop.

"Mrs. Prosser, would you?"

The bishop looked at Mrs. Prosser and shook his head. Mrs. Prosser returned his glance and got to her feet. She walked past him defiantly, stepped in front of Father Britt and stood beside the picture pointing and smiling.

"Please, Mrs. Prosser, don't smile. This is supposed to be a serious picture."

Mrs. Prosser looked serious.

When the picture-taking was finished, the bishop stepped forward. "I suggest you all return to your seats," he said. "And we'll continue—unless you have more questions. You'll all get an opportunity to examine the picture when we're finished. Now, any questions?"

"Father Britt, where did the picture come from originally?"

"It was bought twelve years ago," said Father Britt. "It was bought from a religious supply house as were all the other pictures and statues in the church and rectory. It is a very common picture. I daresay there is one like it hanging in every rectory in the country. Perhaps throughout the world."

"Is that the original frame?"

"No. The glass was broken several years ago when it fell from the wall and I replaced the frame and the glass with a frame from the ten-cent store."

"Why are the eyes closed, Father? Isn't that unusual in a picture?"

"Not at all. There are many such pictures. It is a very common likeness. Perhaps His Grace can give you the historical background on why the picture has closed eyes. I don't know why."

Nobody raised a hand. The bishop waited a full minute and then was about to step forward to close the press conference when a hand went up in the rear of the recreation room.

"Yes," said Father Britt.

Herman Wekstein got to his feet. "I have a question, Father Britt," he said.

"What's he trying to do?" whispered the bishop.

"He's asking a question. What is your question, sir?"

"We've heard the Bishop's opinion of what he calls 'the incident.' I wonder, Father Britt, if you'd care to tell us your opinion? On or off the record." Herman Wekstein sat down.

"I don't think my opinion has any importance in this particular case," said Father Britt.

"You afraid of the Bishop, Father?" asked a reporter in the first row. "He won't bite you, will you Bishop?"

"I just don't feel my opinion has any value, weight, or importance."

"Why don't you let us decide that, Father? Go ahead, we'd like to hear your opinion."

"All right," said Father Britt.

Biff Rogers poked Herman Wekstein in the arm. "What are you and your friend trying to do?" he asked. "Throw the ball game?"

"I think everything the Bishop has said here today is valid," Father Britt continued. "I am as aware as he is that there is actually very little specific evidence of a miracle in this particular case. If I were a judge and this evidence were presented to me, I would throw the case out of court. If I approached the events logically, I would have to admit, along with the Bishop, that there is very little reason to believe in either the supernatural or the miraculous in the case of Rickie Prosser's vision and the moisture on the picture. Both can and, I suspect, will be explained away and dismissed. However, I am not a judge, I am not approaching the evidence with a slide rule. What is rational about the immaculate conception? But I believe it! What is rational about the miracle of the Mass, turning bread and wine into the body and blood of Christ? But I believe it! What is rational about the Holy Ghost, the Holy Trinity and the ascension of Christ into heaven? But I believe them! All of them. I believe. I am a seventy-two-year-old Irish Catholic priest. Many years ago I chose this vocation . . . or was chosen for it. I am a priest. I am a Catholic. I believe. If I did not believe in miracles, I would long since have renounced my Holy Orders and found another way of spending my life."

Father Britt paused. There was not a sound in the auditorium.

"It is not too difficult to be a Sunday Catholic," he went on. "It is not too difficult to come to church once a week, go to confession once a month, receive Holy Communion, abstain from eating meat on Fridays, keep the Holy Days of Obligation, relegate religion to one section or segment of one's life. It is not too difficult. To a priest, being a Catholic is slightly different. He is a weekday, seven-day a week Catholic. And like the rest of you, I'm subject to depression, self doubts and boredom. It is a terrible thing, gentlemen, to reach the age of seventy-two, without certainty setting in solid. Perhaps like Rickie Prosser, I believe because I want to believe. Perhaps I very selfishly accept this incident as a very personal miracle. A miracle for myself. I see it, in terms of myself, as a sign . . . an affirmation of what I have devoted my life to. I don't care what the investigation shows. I don't care if the boy admits he was mistaken. I don't care what a laboratory says about the moisture on the picture. I know, in my heart—and more important, perhaps, since I'm a seventy-two-year-old Catholic priest, in my immortal soul—that this *has* an importance. To me. Not to you perhaps, or the bishop. But to me. To answer your question simply. Yes. I accept it as a miracle. A very private, personal miracle. But to me, a miracle."

Nobody said anything after Father Britt had finished talking. Mrs. Prosser started to applaud, suddenly remembered that to all intents and purposes she was in church and stopped herself. The bishop cleared his throat.

Biff Rogers leaned over and whispered to Herman Wekstein. "Your friend, the priest, is going to wind up with the church equivalent of pounding a beat in Canarsie."

Father Britt sat down.

"Thank you, Father Britt," said the bishop, "for that very personal, and I might add, emotional reaction. It was very eloquent and I realize I should have availed myself of the opportunity of hearing your sermons more. However, I think it really has nothing to do with what we are discussing here. I am impressed by your piety, if not your logic. I am impressed by your honesty, if not your prudence. I am not sure at all that your remarks have made any contribution to the discussion. Now, are there any more questions?"

Father Britt stood up.

"Yes, Your Grace," he said. "I have a question."

The Bishop glared at him. "I was speaking to the newspapermen, Father Britt," he said. "Any questions you may have for me can be discussed in private."

"Let the priest ask his question," shouted a reporter in the back row.

The other reporters took up the chant.

Bishop O'Leary held up his hand for silence. "All right, Father Britt," he said. "Ask your question."

"It's a very simple question, Your Grace. It concerns the picture. How do you explain the fact that the moisture just happened to form at the corners of both eyes and nowhere else on the picture?"

"Pure chance. Coincidence."

"Chance? Coincidence? Why only at the corners of the eyes? Why not somewhere else on the picture as well? Let's assume for a moment that it is perspiration or perfectly normal moisture. Why only in those two places, Bishop? Why not on the chin or on top of the head? Why only in the corners of the eyes? And why both eyes? Isn't that a little too pat for mere chance, Your Grace?"

"It's unusual, I'll admit, but not altogether outside the realm of possibility."

"Possibility, Bishop? Are you a gambling man? Do you have any knowledge of odds?"

"I'm an auxiliary bishop of the Catholic Church," said the bishop, pompously. "I know nothing about gambling or odds.

"The odds, Your Grace, of the moisture appearing only in those two places would be something like five million to one . . . just short of an impossibility."

"And what does that prove?" thundered the bishop. "What does that prove,"

"It proves, Your Grace," said Father Britt in a quiet voice, "that the picture incident is not as cut and dried as it might appear at first glance."

"I think, Father Britt, you are overstepping your authority. Those are questions that, quite rightly, should be covered in the investigation."

"I'm pointing them out, Your Grace, on the off chance that they might be overlooked in the investigation."

"And what do you mean by that?"

"Precisely what I said."

"I think we've about covered everything," said the bishop, staring at Father Britt. "Gentlemen, unless you have any further questions I think we can consider this press conference adjourned."

Three hands were raised in the auditorium.

The bishop turned his back on the audience and left the stage. Father Britt, carrying the picture, prepared to join him.

"Good for you, Father," whispered Mrs. Prosser.

"Thank you, Mrs. Prosser," said Father Britt, ruffling Rickie Prosser's hair. A cameraman caught the picture and Father Britt nodded to everyone and left the recreation room.

When he got back to his study he found the bishop, Herman Wekstein, and Biff Rogers waiting for him. Mrs. Doody had put a silver coffee pot and the accessories on the desk. Father Britt poured himself a cup of coffee . . . offered it around and then proceeded to drink it slowly, himself.

This is going to be it, he thought. For the Love of God, Father Britt, he thought, keep your temper.

There was no doubt in anybody's mind that the bishop was mad. Good and mad. "Just exactly what did you think you were doing down there?" he asked.

"Taking part in a press conference," said Father Britt.

"Looked to me," said Biff Rogers, "like you were bucking for priest of the year."

"Biff, please. Let me handle this," said the bishop. "You realize, of course, that you succeeded in holding your bishop up to ridicule before the members of the press?"

"That was not my intention."

"I don't care what your intention was. That's what you

did. Look, Father Britt, I know you don't like me . . . never have. That doesn't matter. I am a bishop and by the Holy Mother, you will show me some respect in public. Odds! I might have known you'd be an authority on that!"

"Men," said Herman Wekstein, "are authorities on a great many things that have nothing to do with the way they earn their living."

"Mr. Wekstein and you too, Biff . . . would you mind leaving us alone? What Father Britt and I have to say to each other is, perhaps, better said in private."

Herman and Rogers left, reluctantly.

"And," shouted the bishop after them, "keep Father Kincaid out there with you, if he ever returns."

"I'm very sorry, Your Grace," said Father Britt when they were alone. "I had no intention of holding you up to public ridicule or getting involved in an argument with you."

"I have no interest in your intentions, Father Britt. Just who do you think you are? You have doubts? Good God, man, do you think you're the only priest who has ever had doubts? Don't you think all of us . . . and that, I suspect might even include the Holy Father . . . have doubts, once in a while. But we don't parade them in public. Certainly not from a stage at a press conference."

"Hadn't the odds of the moisture appearing just where it did occurred to you, Your Grace?"

"Of course it occurred to me. All the brains and logic in the Church are not confined to parish priests, Father Britt."

"I have a certain vested interest in this matter, Your Grace."

"I know," said the bishop, sarcastically. "You're seventy-two years old. You're Irish. You're a Catholic. You're a priest. You're a-seven-day-a-week Catholic. I heard all that. Now you listen to me, Father Britt. You butt out of this situation, do you understand?"

"Are you threatening me, Your Grace?"

"If you want to think so."

"What are you threatening me with? Excommunication? Taking me out of St. Martin's? As you just reminded me, I'm seventy-two years old. Do you think threats worry me?"

"Father Britt, it may come as something of a surprise to you, but you are where you are as an object of charity. Normally you'd have been relieved of your parish long long before this and put into some unimportant corner of the Church hierarchy to live out the rest of your days. Charity, Father Britt. Christian charity. Don't you think I know how you've been running this parish? Don't you think I know about your handicapping? Odds! You certainly do know the odds. You're an old horse player masquerading as a priest!"

"Your Grace," said Father Britt, "this is my church. This is my rectory. This is my study and I'm asking you now to get out of it."

"You are, are you?"

"Yes, I am. Go ahead. Go back to your town house in your Cadillac. Remove me. Put me in a corner to live out my days. But until you do, remember that this is still my parish."

"And I suppose when you do leave, the first thing we'll discover is that you've been dipping into the collection and the parish funds to bet on your horses."

"How dare you?" cried Father Britt. "How dare you say that to me?" Father Britt clenched his fist and took a step forward.

The bishop, involuntarily, backed up and as he did so he brushed against the picture Father Britt had brought back from the recreation room. It fell to the floor and the glass cracked. The bishop bent down to pick it up.

"Holy Mary, Mother of God!" he said.

Father Britt bent down beside him.

Two drops of moisture had formed at the corners of the eyes, and as they watched, the drops rolled across the face and fell on the floor.

"Father," asked the bishop, "do you see it too?"

"Yes, Bishop O'Leary. I see it."

"The eyes did not open, did they?"

"No, Your Grace, the eyes did not open."

"Thank God for that," said the bishop.

The bishop and Father Britt agreed not to say anything to anyone else about what they had seen. When the bishop left, he took the picture with him, in Biff Rogers' dispatch case. After that Father Britt and Father Kincaid played cribbage, first removing the phone from the hook. They both went to bed early. However, the Prossers entertained a reporter from the *Journal-American* who gave them a check before he left.

MONDAY

FATHER Kincaid was up at dawn, and was sitting in the parlor reading his breviary when Father Britt came in.

"If you don't mind, Father Kincaid," he said, "I think it would be a good idea for you to say the morning Mass."

"I'd be delighted, Father," said Father Kincaid closing the book and getting to his feet. He made no mention of the fact that Father Britt was wearing a tattered, faded bathrobe that had once been bright blue and a scuffed pair of house slippers. Father Britt yawned and scratched himself on the shoulder just below a large moth hole.

"You must have had a very tiring day, Father," said Father Kincaid.

"Nothing of the sort. And I have no intention of going back to bed if that's what you have in mind. I've had plenty of sleep.

"I meant no harm by it, Father. I just thought that at your age . . ."

"At my age!" thundered the older priest. "Since when

has a priest's age had anything to do with his competence? What am I, a relief pitcher? A jockey? A movie star? At my age! Let me tell you something, Father Kincaid, at my age I could say the Mass standing on my head."

"I meant no harm by it, Father Britt."

"Then why did you say it?"

"It was just . . ." Father Kincaid blushed. "I'll get ready for the seven o'clock Mass now, Father, if you'll excuse me," he said with dignity.

Mrs. Doody chose that moment to walk into the parlor. "And what'll you be having for breakfast this morning, Father?" she asked.

She always started the day by asking the same question and Father Britt was certain that if he'd turned to her and said butterfly knees and roast grasshopper she'd have smiled and said, "Of course, Father, bacon and eggs, toast and coffee . . ."

"I wish you'd remember, Father, to give me that bathrobe for mending. There's a big moth hole in it. It would be a Christian charity for you to buy yourself a new one . . . Now will you be having your breakfast, Father?"

"No," shouted Father Britt. "No I will not!"

Mrs. Doody retreated a few steps and Father Britt softened his bellow by adding, "A little later Mrs. Doody, thank you. Not now."

Mrs. Doody nodded and for a moment Father Britt was afraid that she was about to burst into tears. She'd done that once many years ago and it had bothered the old priest until Herman Wekstein explained that women frequently get difficult at certain points in their lives and even a priest's housekeeper wasn't immune to the inevitable inroads on

112

the nerves of the passing years and biological changes in the human body.

"Are you feeling all right this morning, Father?"

"Of course I am."

"Those chest pains haven't come back? Your back feels all right?"

"Why this sudden interest in my health? Father Kincaid is ready to give me Extreme Unction because I let him say the mass this morning. Now you stand there and look at me as if you're about to light a candle for my immortal soul."

"Well, Father, you'll admit things haven't been exactly normal around St. Martin's these last couple of days. And then to have you come out like that . . ."

Father Britt became aware of his costume.

"Oh . . . well . . ." he said. "I wanted to tell Father Kincaid that he was to say Mass and I saw no reason to dress myself to do that. Do you understand, Mrs. Doody?"

"Oh yes, Father. I meant nothing by it."

The phone rang and Mrs. Doody went into the hall to answer it. She returned with something resembling awe on her face.

"It's the bishop," she said.

"The bishop? At this hour?"

"That's what he said. 'This is Bishop O'Leary,' he said. 'I would like to talk to Father Britt.' "

"How does he sound Mrs. Doody?"

"Like the voice of God."

"I mean besides that. Does he sound affable, annoyed, or petulant?"

"He sounds like Bishop O'Leary. Do you think you should

keep him waiting, Father?"

Father Britt shuffled out into the hall and picked up the phone.

"Father Britt speaking," he said.

"This is Bishop O'Leary. Are you all right?"

"I don't know what this sudden interest in my health means. I'm fine, Your Grace. Had a wonderful night's sleep. Feel top of the morning."

"Father, have you seen the morning newspapers?"

"No, Your Grace. Should I?"

"They played the story up very big. Wait a minute. Here they are. The *Daily News* has a picture of both of us on the front page and a headline that says 'Bishop Doubts Miracle.' The *Mirror* has the same picture and the headline says 'Church Investigating Miracle of Crying Picture.' The *Herald Tribune* has it in the lower left-hand corner of page one. The headline says 'Church Adopts Wait-and-See Policy on Crying Picture.' The *Times*," continued the bishop, a note of regret creeping into his voice, "buries the story on page twenty-seven. The entertainment section. However, I understand from Biff that it will get a big play in the afternoon papers. Now, Father Britt, listen to me."

"I'm listening, Your Grace."

"I sent the picture off to the laboratory. Do you have any extensions at the rectory?"

"Two."

"Would you check and make sure nobody is listening on them?"

"That won't be necessary, Your Grace. I can hear Mrs. Doody in the kitchen, whistling."

"What?"

"Rose of Tralee, I think."

"Rose of what?"

"Tralee."

"What are you talking about?"

"You wanted to know what Mrs. Doody was whistling."

"Why would I want to know that?"

"I'm sure I don't know, Your Grace. Rose of Tralee. I'm sure of it."

"Father Britt, will you stop this foolishness! Now you're sure nobody is listening in on any extension?"

"Positive."

"Now listen to me. I sent the picture to a testing laboratory when I left you last night. They agreed to do the tests immediately and send me the results as soon as they finished. I have those results in my hand now."

The bishop paused. Father Britt said nothing. "Are you there, Father Britt?"

"Of course I am, Your Grace."

"Don't you want to know what the results were?"

"I'm sure you'll tell me."

"Are you sure you're feeling all right? You know a man of your age . . ." The bishop laughed mirthlessly. "After all," he continued, "none of us is getting any younger. I'm fifty-one, myself."

Fifty-five, corrected Father Britt mentally.

"Anyway," said the bishop, "here are the results. I might add that this is a completely reliable laboratory. Several of the large cigarette concerns use its facilities for test purposes. 'We have found the moisture,' they say, 'to be of an oily nature which could not be said to resemble human tears.' You hear that, Father Britt? *Could not.*"

"Nobody suggested they were *human* tears, Your Grace," said Father Britt.

"Let me read the rest of it: 'The liquid tested contained only a trace of sodium chloride, one of the major elements of human tears and no nitrogenous compounds, usually found in tears. It probably was a watery liquid on the picture, but when we received the picture to test it, only residue was left. A more accurate test could be made if a hypodermic needle was used to get the substance. It is our further suggestion, because of the oily substance, that the moisture was the result of repeated exposure of the picture to direct sunlight or possibly its location near a source of artificial heat.' "

"Is that the end of the report?"

"Yes."

"And what conclusions are you drawing from the report?"

"Only the conclusions the report itself draws, Father Britt. The picture has been hanging in the sun for a long time, hasn't it? There is a radiator in the room close by the picture, isn't there?"

"And you feel that explains it?"

"I don't know. I honestly don't know. I suggest that you go out and purchase a hypodermic needle."

"A hypodermic needle, Your Grace? Why should I do that?"

"Well . . . for some reason these things seem to be happening in your church. On the off chance that something similar happens, I'd want you to collect the evidence for the laboratory with a hypodermic needle."

"All right, Your Grace."

116

"I dare say this whole thing isn't over yet, Father. Rogers advises me to sit tight and not give the newspapers anything to help keep the story alive. My line with them is very simple. An investigation is being made and until it is completed there will be no further, official Church announcements. Rogers feels that silence is the best solution. He feels that unless there is another incident the whole thing will be forgotten and dropped in a couple of days."

"By another incident he means something like the picture crying again? For the second time?"

"Yes, something like . . . Oh, I see what you mean." The bishop lowered his voice.

"You haven't mentioned that . . . second incident to anyone, have you?"

"Of course not, Your Grace. I gave you my word. You're not doubting the word of a priest, are you?"

"Of course not, Father. You know, you may be doing me something of an injustice. Don't forget that I'm a priest as well as a bishop. You may not think so, Father Britt, but I can assure you that I am just as devoted to my God and my religion as you are. There may be administrative and nonpastoral duties that concern me a great deal, but I am also a Catholic priest. I am not trying to hide anything or cover anything up.

"I do, however, have a responsibility you do not have— a responsibility not to let this incident or any incident like it be blown out of proportion and turn into a sideshow. Besides, Father Britt, you know as well as I do that if this thing blows up again I'll have to buck it upstairs to the Cardinal. You know how emotional he can get about things like this. I'd like to keep it under control just between us.

That's why I'm asking you to get yourself a hypodermic needle, just in case, and to say nothing about what we both saw yesterday afternoon. And if the press comes around to see you, say nothing beyond the fact that an investigation is under way. Do I make myself clear?"

"Yes, Your Grace. Very clear."

"Then see that you give me no cause to repeat it."

Father Britt hung up the phone. He spent a good part of the rest of the morning on his knees. He was thoroughly ashamed of himself. He knew that one of his great and repeated failings was his inability to obey one of the major commandments of his Church and his religion.

He had never felt the slightest desire to covet his neighbor's goods or wife. He had never stolen, worshiped false gods, borne false witness, committed murder, or failed to honor his father and mother. He had, however, always found it difficult to follow literally the admonition to love his neighbor as himself.

He frequently found his neighbors to be bores, to smell bad (as age weakened his other faculties, Father Britt found his sense of smell sharpening), or to make outrageous demands on his time, patience and temper. Not loving your neighbor was bad enough for an ordinary man. Purgatory must be full of sinners who hadn't quite been able to do it. But for a priest to feel that way was a terrible sin. And where in the name of the Holy Mother would they put a priest who couldn't find it in his heart to love his bishop? Surely if loving a neighbor was important enough to rate Commandment status, loving a bishop must take precedence over that. Or was it really that serious? He had heard enough people confess the resentment they felt against

118

their boss or their immediate superior to recognize that the resentment was basically a human, if sinful emotion. Was that all it was in his case? Did his advanced age feed his resentment of a superior many years his junior?

No. It wasn't that at all. It was sinful and wrong.

He prayed for guidance and help. He knew in his heart that his prayers were doomed from the start by the words in which he couched them. "Help me, Oh, Lord, to love that sanctimonious, opinionated, egocentric idiot, Bishop O'Leary."

That was certainly not the way to approach God in this particular case.

On the other hand, it didn't seem right to ask for guidance in loving that wise, good, intelligent man of God, Bishop O'Leary. Certainly God would have as little patience with that sniveling, dishonest approach as with the other. Herman Wekstein had reminded him once that you can't con God.

As a young priest he remembered being concerned with whether God had a sense of humor. He had pored over the Bible, the catechism and the Catholic dogma for some evidence of it.

After all, he argued, hadn't the bishop himself just reminded me that he was also a Catholic priest? Do I doubt his sincerity, his belief, his commitment, his whole commitment to the Church and its precepts.

No.

But couldn't he be a bit less autocratic, a little less ridiculous? A little less arrogant and sure of himself? A little more human?

Father Britt's knees began to pain him and he had a

cramp in his thigh. A little longer, he thought. The fact that he was aware of his physical discomfort convinced him that he was not approaching his God in a proper frame of mind. He tried again, tried to dismiss the pain in the knees, the cramp, the pounding noise in his eardrums and the slight feeling of nausea and dizziness. He reluctantly got to his feet, went to his room, dressed and came out to find his breakfast waiting for him on the table.

"Are you all right, Father?" asked Mrs. Doody.

"Of course I'm all right."

"You haven't been to the newsstand this morning, Father."

"That reminds me, Mrs. Doody. Call Herman Wekstein and find out where he put those pictures he took off my walls. We must all sail under our own true colors, Mrs. Doody. Even a priest."

"I know where he put them, Father. I've already got them back on your wall."

"Where were they?"

"In the filing cabinet. Filed under P, for pictures."

"Shows you, Mrs. Doody," said the priest, starting on his bacon and eggs, "what an insight into the mind of a man a filing cabinet has. I'd have filed them under H, for horses. You'd have filed them under W, for winners. Bishop O'Leary would have filed them under S, for sin . . . and all they are, after all, Mrs. Doody, are some rather good pictures of one of God's noblest creatures."

Mrs. Doody, having dealt with Father Britt's morning moods for a quarter of a century smiled and said, "Yes, Father," and proceeded to pour cream into his coffee cup. "Father Kincaid said the seven o'clock Mass was jammed."

120

"I'm sure it was."

"Father, with all the excitement, with the newspapers all over the place and the bishop, I don't suppose you got a chance to check your Saturday selections, did you?"

"No, Mrs. Doody, I didn't. But somehow I feel you did."

"Indeed, I did, Father. You had four winners, including Melissa's Husband. One of the best days you ever had."

"In that case, I assume the meals will improve this week."

Mrs. Doody said nothing.

Father Britt finished his breakfast in silence. When he walked through the hall toward the street, Father Kincaid had already started on his round of sick calls and Mrs. Doody was busy cleaning up the vestibule and the hallway. He had his second cup of coffee in the coffee shop on the Avenue, talked to Willie Brandt, watched the garbage truck grind up its daily offering from the galvanized cans in front of the tenement and headed for Herman Wekstein's drugstore. Herman was sitting at the soda fountain drinking a large glass of seltzer water.

"Good for gas," he said. "If you have it, it brings it up. If you don't have it, it gives it to you. A real smart man could call it a miracle drug for indigestion and make a fortune. Forgive me, Maurie, I should use the dirty word 'miracle.' Any pictures crying this morning?"

"Please, Herman, no jokes this morning."

"You're late, Maurie. The excitement too much for your old Irish heart?"

"Please. Not you too. Suddenly everybody in the world is asking how I feel. I feel fine!"

"Good. Come in the back. I'll give you a glass of tea.

121

Maybe a bagel."

"Not this morning."

"Why suddenly not this morning? You getting too important for a glass of tea and a bagel now that you have your picture on the front page of the *News?* Now that you have usurped the natural habitat of the movie star and the child murderer, the victim of the auto accident and the grief-stricken parent you can't bother with your old friends?"

"Herman, I came to buy something."

"Now that is a miracle."

"Herman, please. No jokes. Not this morning."

"Are you feeling all right?"

"Fine, I told you. Fine. Now stop asking. I'm fine."

"Do you mind if I make a guess, Maurie? Sit down, try some seltzer. Two cents plain we used to call it. It's the Jew's holy water."

He went behind the counter of the fountain and pulled the spigot and poured a large glass of seltzer water. Father Britt accepted it, looked at it dubiously and swallowed the whole thing in one gulp. He belched. Looked surprised and smiled.

"It works, doesn't it?" he said.

"You doubted it? What's the matter, Maurie? The bishop climbing up your back?"

"What makes you think that? All right, Herman. His Grace was on the phone this morning. At seven o'clock. Do you know what it means to have a bishop on the phone at seven o'clock?"

"I think the last time it happened was during the San

122

Francisco earthquake. Have a little Christian charity, Maurie."

"Don't you think I'm trying? I've worn calluses in my knees this morning praying for a little Christian charity toward the bishop. Herman, I'll tell you the truth. I can't find it in my heart to be charitable toward him. I can't. And there's no use saying I can. I know it's wrong and sinful, but I can't. This isn't something to be manipulated, Herman. I don't know whether it's a miracle or not. One minute I think it is, the next minute I'm not so sure. The next minute I'm sure it isn't. But it is something serious to be investigated and questioned and approached with care. It is not something to manipulate or dismiss or ignore. It is not something to be hushed up . . . or exploited either."

"Maurie, have some more seltzer."

Herman poured out another glass of seltzer and handed it to the priest. He drank it slowly.

"A good belch never hurt anyone," said Herman. "Let me tell you something about your bishop. He is a confused man. There is one side of him that wants to grab hold of this miracle of yours and press it to his chest. Don't forget something else, Maurie. He is a member of your Church, too. I can't believe he has spent his life as a priest and now a bishop because he likes the uniform or the hours. He believes too, Maurie. Will you grant him that?"

"I'll grant him that."

"All right. Then there is another side of him that inhabits a world that is closed to most priests. He's an accepted citizen in the world of the celebrity. He is one himself. He lunches at "21" a couple of times a week. He goes to the opening of plays. He travels around in a chauffeur-driven Cadillac. He can talk the mumbo jumbo of the advertising and television people. He has both worlds, Maurie. And he has a big solid feeling of guilt because of it.

"He justifies the actresses he lunches with because every once in a while he converts one of them. He justifies the fact that he is a celebrated person and not a simple man of God preaching in the wilderness by claiming that he is a man of his times, using modern methods to spread the Gospel. There is enough truth in that point of view to quiet the guilt temporarily. Enough to allow him to continue doing it. Enough to keep him from being ashamed as a priest of his fondness for luxury, French sauces and the company of the fashionable, the rich and the famous.

"Now you and your crying picture have thrown him into a tailspin. One side of him—the priest side—leaps toward believing it, just as you leap toward believing it. It seems to me, Maurie, that a man like you who dedicates his life to religion would have no real trouble accepting the reality of any miracle. Your whole religious faith is based on miracles. What is so special about a small miracle like a crying picture? Why shouldn't you believe it? Why shouldn't the priest that has become Bishop O'Leary believe it?

"But then the conflict comes into it again, Maurie. The other side. The celebrity, the man who knows all the answers, who plays the match game and knows headwaiters by name and the best vintage years of wines . . . the man who would hate anyone to call him a square. The man they all say is a sensible churchman and not always stuffing religion down their throats . . . who takes a drink now and then, who argues morality with Tennessee Williams and argues Church history with a Zen beatnik in a coffee shop.

"Your little miracle, Maurie, has caught your bishop between two worlds and he has to decide which is his real world. As a churchman he must always accept the possibility of it being genuine. As a citizen of the expense-account places, he wouldn't be caught dead being so naïve or so ingenuous. A little Christian charity for the bishop, Maurie. A little more seltzer?"

"No, thank you, Herman. You know something?"

"What, Maurie?"

"Herman, you'd make a very good priest."

"Thank you, Maurie. I've always said you'd make a good druggist. I don't mean that like a smart aleck, either. In a way we're in the same business. Sometimes my aspirins and lipsticks do as much good as your confessions and Masses."

"Don't spoil it."

"I'm not spoiling it. Come in the back, have a glass of tea and a bagel."

"I really can't. I came to buy something."

"That's right. I'd forgotten. Now, what magic nostrum can I give you?"

"A hypodermic needle."

"Maurie! You've become a drug addict?"

"Herman, please. No jokes."

"May I ask why you want this particular piece of merchandise?"

"To catch tears." Father Britt smiled. The smile became a laugh. The laugh became hysteria. The hysteria wound

125

up in a coughing spell. Herman Wekstein pounded him on the back and the cough, the laugh and the hysteria disappeared.

"We have several sizes," said the druggist. "Are these small tears or large tears?"

Father Britt laughed again. He managed to control it this time. "Just ordinary run of the mill tears from a picture," he said.

"We have a special on those this week," said Herman. "It's been a big week for picture tears."

Father Britt told Herman the full story of the bishop's morning phone call and the further he got into it the funnier it seemed to him. He finished by quoting the laboratory report and the bishop's request that he arm himself with a hypodermic needle . . . just in case. Herman said not a word during the recital and when Father Britt had finished the druggist went to the rear of the store and returned with a box containing a large hypodermic needle.

"Use it in good health, Maurie," he said handing it over.

"You think it will happen again, Herman?"

"Yes, Maurie. I think it will happen again. Any new revelations from the Shakespeare of the tenement hallways?"

"Rickie? I haven't seen him since the press conference yesterday afternoon."

"I think you will be hearing from him again too, Maurie."

"Why do you say that?"

"It's like the flying saucers. Once you've seen one you'll see lots more. Just as you'll find a whole rash of crying pictures now that yours has landed on the front pages of the tabloids. Lithographs will spout water like a leaky bucket."

126

"It's already happened again," said the priest quietly. He told Herman the details of the second incident.

"The poor bishop. He actually saw it happen. Poor Bishop O'Leary."

"You may be on the right track, Herman. If I can't quite work up any love for the bishop, maybe I can feel compassion for him. At least that's a step in the right direction.

"It is, indeed," said the druggist. "I suppose you know you're a hero to the neighborhood?"

"Because of the pictures in the papers?"

"Because of an animal you've never seen, called Melissa's Husband. Mrs. Doody passed the word around in your parish. A killing, I am told, was made. Miracles, Maurie, are a little hard to grasp—even by the holy and the devout. Nobody has any trouble grasping a horse that pays $38.40. Everybody expects a priest to be involved with something a little mysterious but a priest who can pick eighteen to one shots with any degree of regularity. . . . Maurie, such a priest could be a mighty bulwark against communism."

"And what would they call me, Herman? St. Maurie of the Pari mutuels?"

"Come on in the back, Maurie. A glass of tea and a bagel . . ."

"No thank you, Herman. I really am late."

Father Britt walked to the corner and stopped at the newsstand.

"Good morning, Father," said the news vendor.

"Good morning."

"You really done it, Father. I mean, ten minutes after the afternoon papers hit the stand I was sold out. But I saved copies for you, Father. I figured you'd want them for your scrapbook."

"Thank you."

"You in trouble, Father?"

"Trouble?"

"With the bishop I mean, the way you stood up to him in front of the reporters, I figured maybe you're in trouble."

"I don't think so," said Father Britt. "Let's just say we had an honest difference of opinion."

"Like in horse racing, Father. Like they say, a difference of opinion makes horse racing. And thanks for that Melissa's Husband. I mean, $38.40. That's something, Father."

"You made a wager?"

"Not much, Father, I'm ashamed to say. I didn't have the faith. I got the word but I didn't have the faith. Two lousy bucks on his nose. I'll know better next time."

The news vendor handed Father Britt the *Racing Form* and the *Morning Telegraph* and copies of all seven of the New York newspapers. He tucked them under his arm and headed back for the rectory.

When he walked into the parlor he interrupted a strange tableau. Mrs. Doody was standing against the wall putting a picture on the hook. It was a replica of the picture of Christ that had fallen on Saturday. A mannish-looking woman with four cameras strung around her neck was perched on the top rung of a ladder looking through the viewfinder of a Rolleiflex. Three young men were placed strategically around the room holding a couple of hundred pounds of lighting equipment. Father Kincaid, pipe lit, was standing at the foot of the stepladder, steadying it and

128

staring with fascination at the lady's footwear . . . gold-and-black sandals with three-inch heels.

"Just move a little to the right, will you, Mrs. Doody? You're blocking my view of the damned picture. There . . . that's good . . . hold it. Hey, Father, stop jiggling the damned ladder, will you?"

Mrs. Doody, seeing Father Britt enter the room, smiled and waved at him.

"*Peer* magazine," she said, "they're taking my picture."

The woman on the stepladder climbed down backward, bumping against Father Kincaid in the process and sending him spinning off balance against the table.

"Sorry, Father," she said.

She came over to Father Britt and extended her hand through the welter of cameras that swung from her neck like a series of intricate pendulums.

"Liza Yankauer," she said. "*Peer* magazine. You're Father Britt?"

"How do you do," said Father Britt.

"I've been assigned to shoot some pictures. Of course I'm not promising anything, but I'd like to follow you around and shoot hell out of you and the church. O.K.? Pete, for God's sake, turn those damned lights off. The wallpaper's faded enough. You other two can just relax for a couple of minutes. You been to China, Father?"

"No, I haven't."

"Too bad. We dig Chinese missionaries. Look, I know it's a pain in the can but it's my job, right? I mean I'll try not to get in your hair or louse up your Mass or whatever it is you do. I'll just follow you around."

"I'm not sure it would be . . ."

"Look, don't let it worry you. We cleared it with your boss. The bishop said go ahead. He's coming over later. I want to re-create the shot of the two of you on the platform at the news conference. The shots they got are lousy. Flat . . . no highlights. You gotta expect something like that from a bunch of damned butchers with speed Graflexes, right?"

Mrs. Doody was still standing, holding the picture against the wall, smiling vaguely in the direction of Father Britt and the photographer.

"You can relax, Sweetie," said Liza Yankauer. "We're not taking any pictures now. The lights are off. That's how you can tell, honey. Get it? Tell her to sit down, will you, Father?"

Mrs. Doody looked as if she was going to cry again. Father Britt went over to her, took the picture out of her hand, and carefully placed it on the nail. It matched exactly the faded outline left by the previous picture.

"Where did you get the picture, Mrs. Doody?"

"I had it in my trunk, Father. They wanted a picture of me putting it up so I got it out. Is it all right, Father? I didn't think you'd mind."

"You did it just right, Mrs. Doody. You heard her. They have the bishop's permission."

"I don't like faking it with this ringer," said Liza, pointing to the picture on the wall. "But O'Leary promised to bring the real crying picture over with him later. What the hell, who can tell the difference? I thought I'd grab a couple of shots with this one while I had the chance."

"Sounds like a good idea," said Father Britt.

Father Kincaid had recovered his balance and his poise

130

and came over to the group. "That's a Rolli," he said. "I used to practice photography as a hobby when I was in the seminary . . ."

"Look, Father," said Liza, "you don't tell me how to take pictures. I don't tell you how to do the Mass bit. Right?"

"I was just being friendly," said Father Kincaid, blushing.

"Sure, I know," said the photographer. "Pardon me for breathing . . . I just get bitchy when somebody comes on with the 'that's a Rolli' routine. How would you like somebody coming up to you saying, 'that's an altar'?"

"Apology accepted," said Father Kincaid, smiling.

"Who said anything about an apology? That, Buster, was an explanation . . . not an apology. Now, Father," she said, turning to Father Britt, "I figure you're pretty busy doing whatever it is you do, so I'll try not to get in your way too much. I'm gonna need some shots of the church itself and maybe somebody could hustle up that kid that saw whatever the hell he saw. I'll need you later, Father, for stock stuff. You know what I mean . . . maybe blessing the food or whatever it is you do . . . maybe putting on the costumes for Mass . . . sitting at somebody's sickbed. You know, background stuff. And, of course, I'll want you with the bishop when he gets here. Meanwhile I'll sort of shoot it by the seat of my pants. I'll give a yell when I need you for something. O.K.?"

"Fine," said Father Britt. "Perhaps Father Kincaid could go along with you to be of any help you might need. Would you, Father?"

"I'd be delighted," said Father Kincaid.

"You behave yourself," said Liza, "and I may teach you

131

how to read a light meter."

"Just one request, Miss Yankauer," said Father Britt. "Please don't put your used flash bulbs in the holy water fount."

"Flash bulbs! Who uses flash bulbs? They're for *mechanics,* Father. What do you think I'm lugging these three clowns with the lights around with me for? All right, men . . . on your feet. Let's go."

The photographer, her entourage and Father Kincaid left.

"Peer magazine," said Mrs. Doody. *"Peer* magazine. Just think, Father, this time next week Cary Grant may be looking at *my* picture."

"Which, Mrs. Doody, is not the slightest bit objectionable in any part."

Mrs. Doody flushed with pleasure . . . or high blood pressure. Or both.

Father Britt carried his newspapers into his den and spent a few minutes carefully rearranging the pictures on his walls. Satisfied with them, at last, he sat down and read the morning papers before concentrating on the *Racing Form* and the *Morning Telegraph.* The papers were exactly as the bishop had described them on the phone. Father Britt thought the pictures on the front pages of the tabloids were taken from a rather unfortunate angle. He looked heavy. Not fat, he told himself. Heavy. It was certainly the angle. And maybe when this whole thing had blown over he could talk the chancery into allowing him to reactivate the parish baseball team. If he was still talking to the chancery.

He turned his attention to the afternoon papers.

The New York *Post* had a huge headline about the incident on its front page. Below the masthead and blue-and-white streamers announcing the publication of the memoirs of a famous Balkan actress and the inside story of the private life of the heavyweight champion's sparring partner there was a headline in big, black heavy type:

MIRACLE?

NO . . . SAYS BISHOP

YES . . . SAYS PARISH PRIEST

The editorial page was headed by the following paragraph:

"Far be it from us, as a liberal, independent newspaper (perhaps the only one in New York) to jump to any conclusions in the case of the crying picture but we must admit to a certain glow in reading the reports on the news conference held yesterday by Bishop William O'Leary. The bishop came out four-square for a wait-and-see policy on the miraculous origin of the incident. A simple parish priest, Father Maurice Britt of St. Martin's, armed only with his faith and his convictions, stood on his two feet, contradicted the bishop and announced that he was convinced it was an authentic miracle. We do not know if the real story behind the crying picture will ever be told but we do feel a warm glow contemplating the simple spectacle of a priest defying his superior because his conscience and his beliefs insist he must. There's a lesson there somewhere for all of us."

Leonard Lyons used the incident as a springboard to tell an involved and slightly obscure anecdote about Jennifer Jones during the filming of *Song of Bernadette*. Earl

Wilson, under a paragraph headed, "Wish I'd Said That," reported that Arthur Murray was reported to have remarked that we've come a long way. Used to be, said Murray, that people cried at pictures. Now pictures are crying at people.

Jimmy Cannon in the *Journal-American,* in a column headed "Nobody Asked Me But . . . ," had a lead item that said, "Notice how the next Hatfield you run into puts the rap on the McCoys." Beneath it, "In a battle between an Irish priest and an Irish bishop, the smart money has to be on the bishop."

Dorothy Kilgallen had a lead item in her column that said Broadway producers would have turned purple with envy if they'd seen the lines outside St. Martin's church Sunday morning at the eleven o'clock Mass. That item served to give the column its headline, which read, "SRO at St. Martin's."

The *Journal-American* had a red streamer advertising the fact that the personal story of Rickie Prosser, the 11-year-old boy who saw the vision at St. Martin's, began on Page 7. Jack O'Brien suggested that David Susskind could find material for one of his specials in the heart-warming story of the miracle of St. Martin's, instead of the tired rewrites of old movies he was so partial to.

The *World-Telegram and Sun* had a feature story on page three, tracing the career of Bishop O'Leary, with excerpts from his sermons. On page one the paper gave the straight AP story on the press conference.

Father Britt put the papers aside with a groan. He had read the stories with a strange feeling of embarrassment. He wondered why.

He wondered why he felt as if the details of a family

quarrel had been made public property. He felt that something fragile and important had been reduced to the level of a one-day sensation, blown up, and in the process had lost its beauty, importance and truth.

I'm sure, he thought, the bishop would explain that the newspaper stories were doing the Church's work. They were propagating the Faith, giving Catholicism a mass audience. And after all, what harm did the stories do?

And hadn't the pictures pointed out to Father Britt the possibility that he might be getting a little heavy? He must be sure and speak to Mrs. Doody about watching his diet. He'd have to cut down on starchy foods, fatty foods and potatoes. Particularly potatoes.

And how he did love Mrs. Doody's mashed potatoes, swimming in butter.

He bunched the papers together, walked to the filing cabinet and put them away in the section (the most populated section) marked "Miscellaneous."

Father Britt returned to his desk and spread out the *Racing Form* and the *Morning Telegraph* in front of him. He got up, sharpened his pencil and tried focusing his attention on the entries and past performances in the first race.

He found it difficult to concentrate. He turned to the back of the paper to look at the chart of Saturday's races. He studied it carefully.

Melissa's Husband had started dead last. He had trailed the pack at the quarter pole, the eighth pole and at the head of the stretch. The cold hard figures of the chart did not quite illuminate the drama of that stretch drive. Father Britt could see it in his mind's eye. The horse, dead last, out of contending, that suddenly spurted ahead, gained on the leaders and crossed the finish line the winner.

Now *that* was a miracle.

The old priest sighed and reached for the pile of papers on his desk. Monday mornings had always been a chore to him. He hated the routine paperwork of parish business and bit by bit, he realized, he had been unloading most of it on the willing shoulders of Father Kincaid. He took the battered portable typewriter out from under the desk and laboriously typed out a letter to the chancery on church stationery. He had written the same letter for the past eleven months. It was a request for an additional permanent priest for St. Martin's parish. Not that Father Britt wanted another priest or found the work load too heavy. It was the principle of the thing.

Eleven months ago one of his priests had been snatched away from him. He was told it was a temporary measure but the liberated priest had never been replaced. He did not think sending the Hungarian refugee priest to perform one Sunday Mass was the solution. Father Britt felt it was a black mark, not against him but against his parishioners. He didn't like the idea of St. Martin's being downgraded to the level of a two-priest parish.

In his letter he pointed out that the area around St. Martin's was growing and with the apartment-house building boom in the side streets, there were approximately six thousand more potential parishioners of St. Martin's than there had been a year ago. He did not mention that very few of the six thousand were Catholics nor that St. Martin's membership had actually decreased in the past twelve months. He pointed out that no other church of comparable

136

size was required to carry on its many activities with only a rector and an assistant rector.

And then in a burst of creativity he added a final paragraph. "With the distinct possibility," he wrote, "that St. Martin's will again field a baseball team in the Parochial League this spring it becomes more and more apparent that this parish needs the services of an additional priest . . . specifically one with an athletic background in college or seminary." He signed his name with a flourish.

Then he picked up Father Kincaid's carefully written report on the collections at the previous day's Masses. He studied the figures and whistled softly. The collections totaled a little over three hundred dollars more than the average figure for a normal Sunday. On an impulse he got up and went to the battered filing case and pulled out a pile of records . . . listing the weekly collections from the beginning of his tenure of office at the church. He discovered that yesterday's collection was the second largest total, topped only by that memorable Sunday twelve years before when St. Martin's baseball team had won the Parochial League pennant. He remembered that he very wisely had combined the Mass, a Communion breakfast honoring the victorious athletes, and a second collection at the door, presumably to buy new uniforms for the team.

He sat down at the typewriter again, reinserted his letter and added a P.S. "You will notice," he wrote, "on the report of Sunday's collections that St. Martin's has broken a twelve-year record. This would seem to be proof of the renewed vitality and interest in the Church in this neighborhood and should underline the necessity of adding another priest to the roster." He crossed out the ward "roster." On

137

second thought he was afraid it might have too sporting a connotation. He substituted "clerical staff." And may God forgive me for a pardonable exaggeration of the truth, he said to himself.

Next he went over Mrs. Doody's household accounts and found a three-cent error. He spent a fruitless hour and a half trying to trace it and finally added at the bottom of the page another listing: "Miscellaneous Parish expenses: $.03." The books balanced and he called Mrs. Doody in and congratulated her. She beamed and went back to the kitchen determined to surprise Father Britt with a lemon meringue pie for dinner.

He checked through the other parish bills and finally reached for the church's weekly calendar of events. He read it through carefully despite the fact that it was exactly like the one he had read the week before . . . and the week before that . . . stretching back through the years: *"Monday*. Ladies' Sodality, Church history class."

He wrote Father Kincaid's name next to that one. Father Kincaid, he reasoned, was fresher from the seminary and wasn't likely to be embarrassed by an overzealous question from a parishioner who had been boning up on Church history. Besides, he'd noticed that Father Kincaid seemed to blossom in the presence of ladies . . . all ladies . . . so long as he was separated from them by being elevated on a stage. Come now, Father Britt, he chided himself, admit it. The Ladies' Sodality and Church history bore you to tears and your age entitles you to a few dispensations . . . particularly since it is possible for you to assign the meeting to Father Kincaid and have valid and good reasons for the choice.

138

"Tuesday afternoon. Communion classes." He wrote "Father Britt" in the margin next to that one.

"Tuesday evening. Adult confirmation classes." He wrote his own name in the margin next to that one, too. Father Kincaid had a tendency to go beyond the catechism and turn the classes into debating societies. Besides, that put him one assignment up on Father Kincaid. He had discovered over the years that it was good to get one assignment ahead early in the week. You didn't feel so guilty that way dumping later and less painless ones on the curate or the assistant rector.

"Wednesday evening. Holy Name Society, dessert and coffee, card party."

He put his name to that one, too. There were one or two men of the parish who understood the fine points of handicapping as well as he did and he always found it stimulating to argue, over the card table, the relative merits of blinders, muddy tracks and apprentice jockeys.

"Thursday evening. Catholic Action Committee." Unhesitatingly he put down Father Kincaid's name. The CAC, as he called it, was Father Kincaid's idea. It gathered together in the church basement once a week all the most articulate and most militant Catholics in the parish to denounce motion pictures, legislation, birth control, international communism, the infiltration of communists into the colleges of America; to debate whether the United Nations was a Christian organization, and whether St. Martin's parish should send a telegram registering its approval of a pending piece of legislation that would limit the second-class mailing privileges of certain sophisticated magazines featuring rather specific color photographs of starlets. In short, it was an

organization that made its weight felt and its voice heard in the larger community outside the walls of the church building.

Father Britt had attended several of the meetings and had found it difficult to hold onto his temper and his tongue. Feeling that it was unseemly for a priest to shout at his parishioners, even the pigheaded ones . . . he turned the meeting and the problems over to Father Kincaid. Sometimes of a Thursday night he could hear voices rising in anger from the recreation room of the church and sometimes he almost caught just a faint whiff of something that his reason told him could not be brimstone.

So much for Thursday, thought Father Britt.

"Friday afternoon. Meeting of the Ladies' Altar Society." Father Kincaid!

The page suddenly began to shake in Father Britt's hands. He closed his eyes, dropped the paper and held the ends of the desk. He felt dizzy and his ears seemed to close in on him so that all he was able to hear was a faint throbbing inside his head. He found it difficult to breathe and took deep gasping breaths. He held himself perfectly still and for a split second debated calling out for Mrs. Doody. The dizziness passed, his breathing returned to normal and he was able to hear again. He had had similar attacks during the past year and this one was mild in comparison with some of the others.

At least, he thought, there was no sudden, sharp pain in the chest this time.

He picked up the list again.

"Friday evening. Bingo."

He wrote "Father Britt and Father Kincaid" in the margin.

140

He loved to call out the numbers and liked the excitement when one of his parishioners rose triumphantly from her seat, shouted a rousing "Bingo!" and advanced to the stage to receive her prize. The legislature had outlawed money prizes, but the fact that a triumphant Bingo crier carried away nothing more exciting than a terra-cotta ash tray or a set of tea napkins did not detract from the drama and excitement of the game. Father Britt loved Bingo and was disappointed because his clerical position prevented him from buying seven or eight cards and waiting breathlessly for the calling of the number that would give him five across, or a picture frame or a full carder.

Father Kincaid was certainly invaluable on Bingo nights. Some of the parish gamblers bought as many as ten cards and Father Kincaid was jumping here and there, verifying winners, selling additional cards and making change like a born streetcar conductor. To be sure, attendance at Bingo games had dropped alarmingly when cash prizes were first withdrawn and merchandise substituted. But it suddenly picked up again, and the following Monday Father Britt noticed that the Nearly New Shop on the Avenue was well stocked with terra-cotta ash trays and sets of tea napkins.

The priest turned his attention to the weekly work load of the clergy. He made the Mass assignments. He was vain enough to reserve the Sunday eleven o'clock Mass—the prestige Mass—for himself. He assigned Father Kincaid to the three marriages scheduled at the church for that week. Father Kincaid was a great favorite with the families of the brides and grooms because of his dramatic reading of the wedding service. He made it sound like something he was improvising himself from a secure footing on a mountaintop.

The baptisms Father Britt assigned to himself

And now he turned his attention to Mrs. Doody's menus for the week. He gave them a cursory glance and initialed them. He knew this was an empty gesture. Mrs. Doody's weekly menus, like the programs of the local movie house, were "subject to change without notice."

He checked the laundry bills, the bills for candles, and cleaning help and checked the assignment of altar boys for the various services. He checked through the organist's selection of hymns and wrote his usual, irritable weekly note on the bottom of the sheet.

"I'm sure," he wrote, "there must be other Catholic hymns besides 'Come Thou Almighty King' and 'Holy God, We Praise Thy Name.' Or are we trying to get these two on the Hit Parade?"

He signed his name with a flourish and reached for the *Racing Form* and the *Morning Telegraph*.

Yes, it seemed to be a normal Monday morning at St. Martin's. To a casual observer of Father Britt's routine there would have been no hint of anything as extraordinary as a vision or a crying picture.

And today Father Britt found the selections of horses relatively easy. By the time he had finished doping the first six races he had been forced only once to descend to flipping a coin to choose between two equally well-equipped horses in the same race.

As he prepared to attack the seventh race, Mrs. Doody knocked on the door and came in.

"Excuse me, Father," she said.

"Yes, Mrs. Doody, what is it?"

"I didn't mean to intrude on you." She pointed to the

Morning Telegraph spread open on the desk. "You know I'd only interrupt you, Father, when you're in the middle of *that* if it was very important."

"Then I take it this is very important?"

"Mrs. Fuller called."

"Mrs. Fuller?"

"The old lady with the broken hip."

"Oh, yes. The one who talks dirty."

"She says she's dying, Father."

"We're all dying, Mrs. Doody."

"Yes, Father."

Father Britt went back to his paper. Mrs. Doody continued to stand in the doorway. Father Britt looked up.

"Yes, Mrs. Doody, what is it now?"

"About Mrs. Fuller, Father. She wants a priest to pay a sick call."

"Why tell me about it? Father Kincaid is taking the sick calls."

"He's busy, Father. He gets very angry if I disturb him."

"And I don't, I suppose?"

"Yes, Father. But *he* means it. The anger, I mean."

"What's he so busy with, Mrs. Doody?"

"He's talking to a vestment salesman."

"A vestment salesman? He knows we can't afford new vestments.

"Yes, Father. He knows that. But he sees them every Monday. He likes to discuss prices and he likes to feel the samples. He says it's good experience for him to know about things like that."

"All right, Mrs. Doody. Let's not interfere with Father Kincaid's self-education or court his wrath. Did Mrs. Fuller

143

sound very sick?"

"She said she was dying, Father."

"From a broken hip?"

"She said she had complications."

"All right, Mrs. Doody. I'll go see her."

"I told her you would, Father."

Father Britt got up from the desk and put a large circle around the entries in the seventh race. On the off chance that Mrs. Fuller might actually be dying he packed the vials of oils and the cotton used in Extreme Unction in his black satchel, left the rectory and walked around the corner to her tenement apartment.

He knocked, was told to come in and entered a railroad flat guarded by a black nondescript mongrel.

"Don't bother about him, Father," said a voice from the bedroom. "He's never seen a priest before. I got him yesterday. Mrs. Perlmutter, my neighbor downstairs, had pups."

The priest walked cautiously around the dog which snapped at him, but suddenly sat down and attacked his fleas with his teeth. Mrs. Fuller was sitting up in bed. The room smelled of camphor and unwashed clothes. A naked bulb hung from the ceiling over the head of the sick woman. She was surrounded by newspapers, banked in pillows, and looked wan and pitiful. She smiled and her bottom dental plate clicked out of place and back in again. She extended a wasted hand and said, "Thank you so much for coming, Father. I'm afraid I'm dying."

"Now, now," said Father Britt. "None of that." Dying are you? he thought. Bored more likely. Taking a hard-working priest away from his *Racing Form*.

"What seems to be the trouble, Mrs. Fuller?" he asked.

144

"I have these terrible pains in my legs, Father. Shooting pains, they are. It's the mercy of God that I haven't gone out of my head from them."

"You have a broken hip, Mrs. Fuller. That might account for the pains."

"It's not only that, Father. I get the most terrible headaches. Right behind my eyes. Terrible. I see little shooting things . . . in all colors. Now you can't tell me that's normal, can you? And I get shooting pains in my side and up my back. And in my private parts, doctor."

"I'm not your doctor, Mrs. Fuller. I'm your priest and I suggest you save the shooting pains in your private parts for your doctor. What's the condition of your soul?"

"I've got shooting pains . . ." she began, and stopped. She smiled again and clicked her upper dental plate at him in an amazing demonstration of versatility.

"I'm dying, Father," she repeated.

"Would you like me to give you Extreme Unction, Mrs. Fuller?"

For a moment there was genuine fright in her eyes. "Oh, no, Father. No."

"If you're dying, Mrs. Fuller . . ."

The dog provided a diversion by loping into the room and jumping on the bed. Mrs. Fuller reached up and smacked him on the rump. The dog yelped, jumped off and retreated to the kitchen casting reproachful glances at the bedroom until his fleas demanded his full attention again.

"Father, what I really wanted to see you about was all the excitement at St. Martin's. I've been reading about it."

Mrs. Fuller dragged the details out of him. She wanted to know if Dorothy Kilgallen or Jim Bishop had been there and

145

whether he had been asked to be the Mystery Guest on "What's My Line."

Father Britt held on to his temper, never brought up the subject of Mrs. Fuller's potential demise nor opened his satchel to bring out the Extreme Unction oils. After a half hour, he got to his feet and prepared to take his leave, casting an eye around to discover the whereabouts of the dog.

"Father . . ." said Mrs. Fuller, "just a minute. I have something to show you. Reach into the top of the closet there, would you?"

Father Britt opened the closet, pushed his hand through a welter of clothes and touched the top shelf. "What is it I'm supposed to look for?" he asked.

"The picture frame . . ."

Under a pile of clothing, two straw hats, and a classified telephone directory, Father Britt found a picture frame. He pulled it out, came over to the bed and handed it to Mrs. Fuller.

"Here," she said, giving it back to him. "Look at it, Father.

Father Britt looked. It was a replica of the picture of Christ that had hung in the rectory.

"Look at it closely, Father," she said.

Father Britt examined the picture. He held it up so that the light from the air shaft hit the picture squarely. He turned it so that the light would not reflect on the glass. There was unmistakable moisture on the face of the picture. Father Britt hastily turned the picture over and examined the back of the frame. The dust and dirt caked in the brown paper sealed to the edges of the frame were clear-cut evidence that it had not been tampered with. He looked at Mrs.

146

Fuller, who was gazing at him quizzically.

"Well, Father?" she said.

"Well what, Mrs. Fuller?" he asked.

"I guess it means that I have a crying picture too, doesn't it?"

"It would look that way, Mrs. Fuller. When did you first notice it?"

"Years ago. I've had the picture a long time, Father. It used to hang there, over the bed. One day, when I was dusting the frame I noticed that the face seemed to be wet. I took it down and looked at it in the light and I saw the moisture . . . right there where you see it, Father . . . in the corners of the eyes. I didn't think much about it. It was a cheap picture, Father. I just put it back on the wall and forgot about it but every once in a while I'd take it down and look at it . . . up close. And every time, Father, there was moisture, right there in the corners of the eyes. It got on my nerves. I finally took it down and put it up there in the closet. I didn't think anything about it until I read the papers. What does it mean, Father? Do you know?"

"No, Mrs. Fuller, I don't know."

"Who does, if you don't, Father?"

Father Britt ignored the question. "Didn't you think it peculiar enough when you first noticed it to talk to somebody about it?"

"I remember I showed it to Mrs. Perlmutter downstairs. She said what could I expect from a picture I only paid a dollar and a half for. Then I read in the papers about that picture of yours and the holy fuss you and the bishop made about it in front of all those newspapermen. I thought of calling them and telling them you weren't so special after

147

all . . . that I have a crying picture of my own."

"I don't think I'd do that, Mrs. Fuller."

"Why not? I'll bet they'd pay something for the story of my picture."

"Mrs. Fuller, I forbid you to mention it outside this room . . . to anyone."

"*You* forbid me! Don't you talk to me like that, Father Britt. I'm a sick old lady. A member of your parish. I'll do as I please. It's my picture. I paid for it."

"I just think too much has been made of the other picture, Mrs. Fuller. Don't you see that if you showed yours now it would keep the whole thing alive?"

"Are you trying to hush up something, Father? Wasn't it you I was reading about in the papers screaming about how the picture was a genuine miracle, arguing with the bishop in front of all those newspapermen? If you can argue with a bishop, why can't I argue with you?"

"Nobody is arguing with anybody, Mrs. Fuller. I'm just asking you not to say anything about your picture at the moment."

"By the time you let me talk about it, it won't be news anymore. Nobody will want to photograph it. Or me. Or pay me for the story of how I bought it and about the first time it cried."

"Now just stop that, Mrs. Fuller. Just stop that nonsense."

"Why is it nonsense if a picture cries on my wall and a miracle if it cries on yours?"

The logic of the question stopped the priest and cooled off his temper. "I'm asking you not to complicate a complicated situation any more than it already is. Now, can I do anything for you, Mrs. Fuller? Would you like me to hear your confession?"

The old lady grinned. Leered. Clicked her dental plates again. "What would an old lady like me have to confess, Father . . . with a busted hip?"

"Sassing your priest, Mrs. Fuller. Vanity and greed. More interested in getting your picture in the paper and perhaps getting some money from a newspaper than in doing a small service to your Faith and your church."

"Now don't go holier than thouing me, Father."

"Mrs. Fuller, you're an irritable old woman."

"You're right, Father, and I'm not going to say a word about my picture until you tell me to. You know why? Not as a service to my Faith or to my church. Because you asked me to, Father Britt. I like you. I was telling Mrs. Perlmutter that you can always trust a priest that plays the horses and doesn't go all mealymouthed in the pulpit in his sermons."

"I do not play the horses, Mrs. Fuller."

Mrs. Fuller smiled. And winked. "Sure you don't, Father. Sure you don't."

"About the picture, Mrs. Fuller . . ."

"Oh, forget the picture, Father. I just wanted some company. So I used it as a conversation piece to keep you here a little longer."

"When did you buy it?"

"A long time ago . . ."

"How long?"

"Maybe ten . . . fifteen years. Paid a dollar and a half for it in that religious store on the Avenue. The man said you'd just bought one like it for the rectory."

"Has it . . . have you seen moisture on it recently?"

149

"I haven't looked at it in over two years. The tears got me nervous so I put it up in the closet. From the dust on it you can see that I haven't had it down in a long time. I didn't even think about it until I read about yours. You really don't think it is a miracle, do you, Father?"

"I don't know, Mrs. Fuller."

Mrs. Fuller looked him in the face for a moment without saying anything. When she spoke again she lowered her voice as if she were afraid of being overheard. "Father, tell me something," she said. "Do you really believe in miracles . . . and all those things?"

"All what things, Mrs. Fuller?"

"Heaven . . . and turning the bread into the body and the wine into the blood . . . and mortal sin and purgatory. Those things."

"Don't you believe in them, Mrs. Fuller?"

"I was asking you, Father. I know you're a priest . . and a good man and all that. But, honestly . . . just between you and me and the dog . . . do you really believe in them?"

Father Britt feigned indignation. He was surprised to discover that he had to feign it. "I'm ashamed of you, Mrs. Fuller. You call yourself a Catholic and ask your priest questions like that. I'm ashamed of you."

"I didn't mean to hurt your feelings, Father," said the old lady. "It's very beautiful and very nice to believe those things but I'm not really sure I do. I'm not even sure I ever did."

"Then why do you keep the overworked clergy of this parish busy running up here with cries that you're dying?"

"It gets lonesome, Father. And who else would come and sit and talk to an old woman?"

150

"You're a fraud, Mrs. Fuller."

"Never said I wasn't. Never said I wasn't. Not like some people."

"All right, Mrs. Fuller. Yes, I do believe in those things. And so do you. And next time invite an old priest up to pass the time of day with you or for a nice cup of tea and don't send him hurrying out of the rectory with his bag full of the oils of Extreme Unction."

"I'm sorry, Father. I do have those shooting pains. You shouldn't talk to me like that. I might be dying, for all you know. Where's your Christian charity? Fine priest, you are."

"That will be enough of that."

"Would you like a beer, Father? I have some in the icebox. You'll find the opener hanging behind the sink."

"Now you're talking like a good Christian member of St. Martin's. I'd love a beer, Mrs. Fuller."

"Open one for me too."

Father Britt walked around the dog, which opened one eye, glanced at him in passing and went back to his snoring. The old priest found the opener and two cans of beer, opened them and carried them back into the bedroom. He sat on the edge of the bed and handed one of the beer cans to Mrs. Fuller. They both drank and talked and finally he got up to go. "May the good Lord bless you and keep you," said the priest.

"Now don't start that again, Father. I wanted your unprofessional company, not your professional services. Must you go?"

"I'm afraid so, Mrs. Fuller."

"Do you play cribbage, Father?"

"Yes."

151

"Would you come and play cribbage with me some time? You can leave the satchel and the oils at home."

"Next time I'll bring my own beer," said Father Britt. He picked up his satchel from beside the bed and prepared to leave. "Good-by, Mrs. Fuller."

When he got to the door she called to him. "Father, you forgot something."

"What?"

"This," she said and extended the picture toward him. "I wouldn't want you worrying," she said. "Worrying if you could trust an old heathen like myself. And listen . . . don't bother bringing the cribbage board or the cards. I have both. And please don't send that Father Kincaid to see me anymore. He's a dreadful bore. Did you know that, Father? A dreadful bore. He hates beer. And I'll bet *he* never heard of cribbage."

Father Britt took the picture from her outstretched hands. He wrapped a newspaper around the frame.

"Mrs. Fuller, thank you," he said.

"You're welcome, Father."

"Just how old are you?" he asked.

"Seventy-nine my next birthday, if I live."

"You'll live. How are your pains?"

"Shooting. Especially in my private parts."

"Mrs. Fuller, women of seventy-nine don't have private parts. They just have glands."

The old woman started to laugh, Father Britt waved at her, stepped around the dog and out into the hall. All the way downstairs he could hear the old lady laughing. I haven't played cribbage in years, he thought. Or had a can of beer in the middle of the day. I might just put Mrs. Fuller on my regular calling list in the mornings . . . somewhere between Herman and the newsstand.

When Father Britt got back to the rectory Mrs. Doody was putting the lunch on the table.

"We didn't know how long you'd be, Father," she said apologetically. "We waited as long as we could."

"I'm sorry," said Father Britt. "I was drinking beer with Mrs. Fuller. Excuse me a minute."

He went into his office and carefully put Mrs. Fuller's picture on the top shelf of the closet. He washed his hands and came back to the table. Father Kincaid got up as he came to the table and Father Britt motioned him down again.

"I've already said grace, Father," the young man told him.

"Fine. I'll say my own." He bowed his head, said a fast grace and picked up his soup spoon.

"Father Britt," said Father Kincaid, "forgive me for interrupting your soup."

"What is it?"

"I wanted to show you these." He reached into his pocket and took out some samples of vestment materials.

"Aren't they lovely?" he asked.

"You making a patchwork quilt, Father?"

"They're samples of some of the newer vestments. I was talking to one of the representatives of the firm. Aren't they lovely?"

"Yes. Lovely. What does that have to do with us?"

"Did you see the breakdown of yesterday's collections? Very impressive, Father Britt. The bishop will be very pleased."

"And you think he might be pleased enough to permit an

expenditure for new vestments?"

"Our vestments are in a disgraceful condition, Father Britt. And now that St. Martin's is such an important church again . . . I thought . . ."

"What makes you think it's an important church?"

"The attendance yesterday, Father. The figures on the collections . . ."

"Father Kincaid, forgive me for sounding patronizing, but let me tell you a few facts of life. St. Martin's, despite the attendance and collections yesterday, is not suddenly an important church. Don't make the hot-dog-stand mistake."

"The what, Father?"

"Forgive me for talking shop, Father Kincaid. It's a parable. Don't be like the man who runs a hot-dog stand on an obscure crossroads in the country. He is satisfied just scraping along on local business. Suddenly a sensational murder occurs in the woods behind his hot-dog stand and the next day tourists from all over the state drive out to get a morbid satisfaction from being at the scene of a crime. They get hungry and his business booms. Now he can do one of two things. He can tell himself that the world has suddenly discovered that he is serving the best hot dogs in the world and has beaten a path to his door. He can then go out and mortgage his home, his car and his life savings to put up a grand restaurant and a two-hundred-unit motel. The second thing he can do is recognize the truth of the situation. Rake in the money while it's coming and realize that a week from now nobody will even remember the place, the hot-dog stand or him. We are like that hot-dog stand, Father. For the moment we are an object of curiosity, morbid interest and publicity. In two weeks' time the picture and the vision will be forgotten and St. Martin's will go back to being what it has been for a good many years . . . a parish that is just this side of being self-sustaining."

"Forgive me, Father, but I don't think your parable really fits this situation."

"Why not?"

"We aren't selling hot dogs, Father. We are selling faith. I'll grant you that some of the people who came to St. Martin's yesterday were idle sight-seers, but I think once they are exposed to the superior brand of Catholicism we offer here at St. Martin's . . ."

"Superior brand of Catholicism!"

Father Kincaid blushed. Father Britt went back to his soup.

"I see nothing wrong with using affirmative salesmanship on Catholicism," said Father Kincaid, looking down at his plate.

"What was that, Father?"

"Forgive me, Father . . ."

For I have sinned, added Father Britt again, under his breath.

"Forgive me, Father," repeated Father Kincaid, "but I see no reason why we shouldn't use some of that extra collection money to improve the facilities of the church."

"It's no use wasting your time on me, Father. No vestments. The bishop wouldn't approve. He'd settle for sackcloth and ashes rather than see this parish go any further into debt."

"I also talked to the stained-glass man," continued Father Kincaid. "He drew me some preliminary sketches."

"Sketches of what?"

155

"Of a likeness of the picture. *The* picture. The bishop couldn't object to that, Father. It wouldn't cost the parish anything. There are a few wealthy parishioners, Father. I thought perhaps we could talk to one of them who has just lost a loved one and get him to underwrite the expense of a memorial window of that sort. It would be very impressive and would attract even more people to St. Martin's. I'm sure, Father, once they come . . . out of curiosity, perhaps . . . or a morbid interest, if you will . . . we can hold them."

"Who else did you talk to, Father Kincaid? You had a very busy morning, didn't you?"

"You never objected before to my taking on some of the more necessary duties of the parish, Father. Of course, if you think I have usurped any of your prerogatives . . . I'll . . ."

"Now take it easy, Father Kincaid. I was not criticizing. I was only asking for information."

"I thought we might put a statue . . . of the Virgin Mary . . . right on the spot where the Prosser boy saw the vision. Forgive me, Father, for being blunt, but it seems to me that some of the older members of the church do not recognize the importance of merchandising an occurrence of this type. We of the church must be always ready to use some of the modern methods of big business. We must, when the occasion demands, become hucksters, perhaps . . . but hucksters with a cause. Hucksters with a purpose . . . Hucksters for God. Hucksters . . . if you will . . ."

Father Britt, having finished his soup, interrupted. "Father Kincaid, I never realized before how very eloquent you are. No wonder I've been hearing such wonderful things about your Catholic Action Committee."

156

"Too many people," said Father Kincaid, blushing a little, "equate a clerical collar with a closed mind. As modern, aware Catholic members of society we are not afraid to look facts in the face and recognize our responsibilities not only as Catholics but as citizens of the world."

"Have you ever said this publicly, Father?"

Father Kincaid flushed a shade deeper. "Actually, it's part of a speech I've been preparing for the CAC meeting this week."

"It will go over very well."

"Thank you, Father."

"I'll mention your suggestions to the bishop the next time I think he's receptive." Which may be never, thought Father Britt.

"Thank you very much, Father," said the young priest.

The two of them attacked the cold meat-loaf sandwiches in silence and Father Kincaid with a nod, asking permission and getting it, lit his pipe as they drank their coffee.

"Will there be anything else, Fathers?" asked Mrs. Doody.

"Nothing thank you, Mrs. Doody," said Father Britt.

"I have some lovely Jell-o out there."

"No thank you, Mrs. Doody."

"You'll be wanting to get back to your work, Father Britt," said Mrs. Doody, after glancing at her wrist watch. Father Britt took the hint and rose.

Father Kincaid excused himself. "I'm off on my sick calls," he said.

"Don't bother with Mrs. Fuller," said Father Britt. "I went to see her this morning."

Father Britt went back into his office and spread the *Racing Form* and the *Morning Telegraph* on his desk.

"A priest's work is never done," he said, as he applied himself to the entries in the seventh race. He finally finished doping all nine races despite many interruptions.

The mother of one of the brides of the week brought her daughter in for some instructions in the facts of marital life. Father Britt fell heir to all these callers because somehow the mothers felt it was slightly indecent for a priest as young as Father Kincaid to discuss sex with their daughters, religiously or not. Father Britt had long since worked out the formula. First he had the mother wait in the parlor. He briefly checked on the prospective bride's knowledge of reproduction, made some high-sounding generalizations about marriage being a physical union as well as a spiritual one and recommended that the young lady see her doctor for the clinical details. Such talks averaged ten minutes and had long since ceased to embarrass the priest.

The photographer from *Peer* magazine called to tell him that the pictures she'd taken had been ruined in the darkroom and there wouldn't be time to take others and still make the next issue. "Frankly," she said, "they're a little doubtful that the story will still be alive for the issue after next. Give my love to that cute young priest. And I'm sorry."

Mrs. Prosser called to find out if Father Britt had any suggestions for investing the money she'd received from the newspaper for Rickie's story of the vision. He recommended United States Savings Bonds.

At four fifteen, Father Britt felt dizzy and had a sudden sharp pain in his chest. He searched through the bottom drawer of his desk and found the bottle of medicine the doctor had given him a year before when he had suffered a very severe attack. He shook it, looked doubtfully at the smoky appearance of the liquid in the bottle and swallowed a mouthful. It tasted like ammonia and for a minute he was afraid he was going to vomit.

He leaned back in the chair and closed his eyes and the dizziness and the pain disappeared. Maybe I should see a doctor, he thought.

For what? What can he tell me that he hasn't already told me? A slight occlusion he'd called it. When you're over seventy you have to expect an occasional pain and a little dizziness, don't you? But for a fleeting moment he felt something he hadn't felt in years . . . the fear of death.

Priests are supposed to be immune to it, he reminded himself. To a priest death is the beginning, not the end. Then why should he suddenly feel the cold draft of death on the back of his neck? Why should he suddenly be afraid? He put the thought away from him as being somehow disloyal to his Church. He forced himself to think of something else. He replayed, in his mind, the baseball game that gave St. Martin's the Parochial League pennant. Death couldn't compete with the life force of that sweet victory and after the last out was made in the bottom of the ninth, Father Britt turned his attention to his race selections and copied them out, on a piece of scratch paper, for Mrs. Doody. Just as he finished the last one, there was a knock on the door and Mrs. Doody herself entered.

"Excuse me, Father," she said. "Have you finished them?"

"Just making your copy, Mrs. Doody. Here you are."

Mrs. Doody took the sheet of paper, looked at her wrist watch and shook her head. "The fifth race must be off by now."

"I'm sorry. It would be a shame if I happened to pick the

daily double, wouldn't it? An artistic shame, I mean."

"Yes, Father, an artistic shame. I can't help hoping, though, that if you have any winners you'll have them in the late races."

"Just for the sake of our reputation? So nobody will suspect that we turn on the radio in the rectory and practice a little past posting?"

"You wouldn't do that, would you?"

"Of course not, Mrs. Doody. You'd better hurry along now or you'll be up against post time for the sixth race."

"That was *something*. Melissa's husband."

"Something, Mrs. Doody."

"Oh, by the way, there was a reporter and a cameraman around, Father. I didn't want to disturb you. Father Kincaid was back from his sick calls, so I turned them over to him."

"Very good. Now if we could just teach you a little Latin, Mrs. Doody, you could replace both of us."

"You shouldn't say things like that, Father. You, the pastor of a Catholic church."

"No, I shouldn't."

Mrs. Doody turned to leave and stopped in the doorway. "I almost forgot, Father. Willie Brandt is outside. He wants to see you. He says it's very important."

"Won't he tell you what it is?"

"No, Father."

"All right. Send him in."

Maybe he's run out of cigarettes, thought Father Britt. Or had an evil thought of the flesh so real that it won't wait for the confessional on Saturday.

Willie knocked at the door and came in. He stood on the threshold, suddenly realized he still had his woolen cap on his head, took it off and, for good measure, crossed himself.

"Come in, Willie."

"Thank you, Father. Just a minute."

Willie disappeared and came back carrying a large soup carton. He walked over to the desk and deposited it on the floor.

"What can I do for you, Willie?"

"Today is trash day."

Looking at the dirt on Willie Brandt's coveralls, Father Britt saw no reason to doubt it. "And?" he asked.

"Trash day, Father. Not garbage day. Every day is garbage day."

With me, added Father Britt under his breath. Every day is garbage day with me . . .

"Mondays and Fridays are trash days, Father."

"And?"

"I have the trash cans in the backyards. The tenants know they're there and they put things that aren't garbage in them. Like an old chair that falls apart. You couldn't put that in garbage, could you? Or like a bedspring you don't want any more. Things like that. So I went back to the yard, like I always do on Monday afternoons to take out the trash. And to . . . you know . . . look through it . . . you know, Father, sometimes people throw things out they don't want but I could use. I find a lot of good things that way. And guess what I found, Father!"

"I haven't any idea, Willie. What did you find?"

Willie reached into the cardboard carton and pulled out something wrapped in an old, torn sheet. "This," he said and dramatically unwrapped it.

It was another picture of Christ.

161

"I mean, I had two feelings when I seen it, Father. I mean, first it was wrong to throw something holy like that in the trash bin. Then I figured I could keep it. It's a pretty picture, Father. I don't have no pictures on my wall. Then I saw it was like the picture you had, Father. The one in the newspapers. The one that cried. *And I looked close at it, Father.* Here, *you* look at it."

Willie thrust the picture at the priest and took a step back. Father Britt looked at it, held it sideways to avoid the reflection of the light on the glass and saw what he expected to see. There was moisture on the face of the picture.

"It's crying, Father. Like yours. I come right away when I seen that. Right away, Father."

"Thank you, Willie."

Willie Brandt crossed himself. "What does it mean, Father? Is it another miracle? Like yours?"

"I don't know, Willie."

"I thought you should have it, Father."

"You were right, Willie. And, Willie?"

"Yes, Father?"

Willie had taken three steps backward and had reached the door. Father Britt had the feeling that he was about to break into a run.

"I wouldn't mention it to anyone, Willie."

"I won't, Father. Who'd believe me, anyway?"

"I'll have to tell the bishop about this, Willie. I'll let you know what happens."

"The bishop?"

"Now remember, Willie, don't say anything to anybody about it."

"I won't, Father. You remember the story about the

162

Protestant you told us, Father? The one about how he went into the church to make fun of Communion and went up to the altar and got the Host and wrapped it in his handkerchief and put it in his pocket to show it off to his dirty Protestant friends. And how he took it out and his handkerchief was full of blood and the blood ran off the Host and down his arm and he fell down dead?"

"I don't think I ever told you that story, Willie."

"Somebody did. I thought it was you. It was somebody, Father. God's truth. Somebody told it to me. It really happened."

"Willie, that's one of those old wives' tales."

"It really happened, Father. God's truth. I remember now, a priest told it to my aunt. She told it to me. That's right, Father. I remember now."

"What does that have to do with us, Willie?"

"I got that same kind of feeling, Father, when I took that picture out of the trash can. And then when I looked close and saw it was crying it just dropped out of my hand. You can see the small crack at the edge of the frame there on the bottom. That's where it dropped out of my hand, Father. I figured you should have it. I didn't want nothing to do with it."

"Yes, Willie, you were right. I should have it."

"And when you tell the bishop, you gonna tell him you got it from me?"

"Of course."

"Would you mind not doing that, Father?"

"Why not, Willie?"

"I don't know. I'd just rather you didn't tell him where you got it."

"All right, Willie. I promise."

"Thank you, Father."

Willie crossed himself, came over to the desk, shook hands very formally with Father Britt, picked up the empty carton and left in a hurry.

Father Britt stared at the picture. While he was looking a new drop of moisture gathered in the corner of one eye and rolled down the face of the lithograph.

He put the picture down on the desk and reached for the phone. He was put through immediately to the bishop.

"Father Britt," said the bishop, "I was about to call you."

"I have two more," said Father Britt.

"Two more what?"

"Pictures. They have moisture on their faces, too."

"Two more!" said the bishop. "I have nine! Worse than that I've had the newspapers on the phone all afternoon. Seems they've received five or six themselves. Father Britt, it looks like your miracle has multiplied. At a conservative estimate, I'd say there are now something like twenty-five crying pictures and probably more to come."

"What does it mean, Your Grace?" asked Father Britt.

He did not realize he was asking the same thing Mrs. Fuller and Willie Brandt had asked him.

"How should I know?" answered the bishop. "I've had to buck the whole thing upstairs."

"All the way upstairs?" asked Father Britt. He realized after he said it that this was a very foolish and dangerous thing to say. The bishop's sense of humor wasn't much to begin with, and it was a safe bet that he wasn't in any joking mood at the moment. Fortunately he misunderstood the question.

164

"All the way," he said. "Right up to the Cardinal. I'm waiting to hear from him now. Listen Father. Please don't say anything to any reporters. Just keep your mouth shut about the whole thing. Buck it along to me. Tell them you're under orders from your bishop. If necessary I'll buck it along to the Cardinal. And don't say anything about those new pictures you have. How many did you say?"

"Two."

"That's nothing. I have nine. No, ten. Another one just came in!"

"Your Grace?"

"Yes, Father?"

"I thought there were some wonderful pictures of you in the papers today."

"They were . . . Listen, Father Britt, let me ask you something. I won't get angry or annoyed. This isn't your idea of some kind of a joke, is it? These pictures? Because if it is . . ."

"Your Grace, please. I can't hear you when you shout."

The bishop lowered his voice, lowered it to something close to a whisper. There was a note of pleading in it. "It isn't, is it, Father Britt?"

"No, Your Grace."

"Good. Good? You know, I'd almost be glad to hear you say 'yes it is,' to admit that it was a practical joke. It wouldn't be a very funny one, Father, but at least it would be some explanation. All right, Father. Remember, you're to say nothing to the papers and if there's anything you should know I'll call."

"Don't call me, I'll call you."

"What?"

"I said if there's anything I should know you'll call."

"That's what I said. Father, why do you have to keep repeating everything I say?"

"I'm sorry, Your Grace."

"You ought to be glad you're just a parish priest, Father. You have no idea! Say a novena that you don't know."

"I will, Your Grace."

"I'll call you, Father. Remember, don't talk to anybody until you hear from me. And you don't have to call and tell me how many more of those pictures have turned up. Good-by."

Ten minutes later Rickie Prosser knocked at Father Britt's door, came in and sat in the chair next to the desk.

"Are you mad at me, Father?" he asked.

"Why would I be mad at you, Rickie?"

"You know . . . the Lady. I seen her, father. I really did."

"I know you did, Rickie."

"Thanks, Father. Can I see the picture again? The one that cried?"

"I don't have it anymore, Rickie. The bishop took it with him."

"Are you gonna be in trouble, Father? Arguing with him that way, like it said in the papers."

"We weren't arguing, Rickie. We just had a mild disagreement."

"Good."

Rickie looked down and saw the paper that had been wrapped around Willie Brandt's picture. He crushed it in his hand and walked around behind the priest and threw it in the basket. Then he saw the picture on Father Britt's desk.

"You said you sent it to the bishop," he said. "I wouldn't have hurt it, Father. I just wanted to look at it."

"This is a different one, Rickie."

The boy looked at it closely. "This one cried too, didn't it?"

"Yes, Rickie."

"That's crazy isn't it, Father?"

"What can I do for you, Rickie? Did you have something on your mind?"

"We got money from that paper, Father. For telling about the Lady. The reporter came and sat down and listened to me and wrote down what I said and then he changed it and they put it in the paper and they paid us money for it."

"I saw it in the paper, Rickie."

"You did, Father? You weren't sore or anything, were you?"

"Why would I be sore?"

"I don't know. Maybe you were thinking like we were hogging it, telling about it in the paper like that. You know, showing off, thinking we were so great. I mean it was your church, Father, and everything."

"No, I wasn't sore."

"Good. You know something? I haven't written a single dirty word on a wall since you talked to me about it. I stopped, like using the Lord's name in vain. Like cursing."

"That's fine, Rickie."

"Mom's gonna give me some of the money. Pop raised hell about it and . . ." The boy stopped and reddened. "I'm sorry. And just after I said I stopped cursing."

"That's all right, Rickie. I'm sure your father did raise hell. Made a damn good try at it, anyway. Now I'm one cuss

167

word up on you, Rickie. Let's keep it that way."

"Sure, Father. You mean priests swear? I don't mean like in the Mass when you have to say "Jesus," or something like that but I mean . . like just now . . . those two words you used."

"Sometimes. There are worse things . . ."

"Sure. But a priest . . ."

"Rickie, you . . . you haven't seen anything else, have you?"

"Like what, Father?"

"Like . . . what you saw in the church?"

"You mean the Lady? No, Father. I just seen her that once. I ain't seen her again, if that's what you mean. I'll bet a person could go through his whole life and never see anything like that even once. I already did. Seen something like that, I mean."

"What did she look like, Rickie?"

"She looked nice. Friendly. She smiled. You know what's funny, Father? Like when I see something scary on the TV or maybe one of those monster movies they have on Saturdays at Loew's . . . I get scared when I get into bed at night. I know they're only stories and they ain't real, but they scare hell out of me. I mean . . . Father . . . they scare me. And here's something that's real . . . the Lady . . . and I wasn't scared at all. How come, Father?"

"She's the Mother of God, Rickie. Why should you be afraid of her?"

"She's like my grandmother. It'd be crazy to be scared of your grandmother."

"Your grandmother?"

"Sure. God is my Father, right? And she's the Mother of

God. That would make her like my grandmother, wouldn't it?"

"I suppose it would."

"Why should I be scared of my grandmother?"

"No reason at all, Rickie."

"Father, what I wanted to talk to you about was this. I told you Mom was gonna give me some of the money to buy a bike. Father Britt, tell me something, will you?"

"What, Rickie?"

"You weren't kidding about that baseball team?"

"No, I wasn't kidding."

"I told Mom. She said you didn't have the chance of a snowball in hell . . . she said there wasn't never gonna be a baseball team at St. Martin's again because the bishop wouldn't give you the money to buy the uniforms. Is that true, Father?"

"Well, there has been some disagreement between the parish and the bishop about St. Martin's fielding a baseball team. And one of the points of disagreement, though not the largest, was the cost of the uniforms."

"You mean Mom was right?"

"Let's say it was a matter of emphasis, Rickie."

"You got the money for the uniforms?"

"Well . . . no, Rickie."

"You do now, Father."

"What?"

"You do now. I'm giving it to you. Who wants a bike, the way Mom makes the rules? You can't ride the bike in the street. 'You can't ride it on the sidewalk. You gotta walk it over to Central Park before you can ride it . . . and walk it back.' What kind of a bike is that, you have to walk it to

Central Park? I want to take the money she's gonna give me for the bike and give it to you, Father. For uniforms for the baseball team. So the bishop can't say no, if you got the money for the uniforms, and I don't have to play for St. Joseph's anymore."

"I don't think it's that simple, Rickie."

"I got a good throwing arm, Father. I hit real good. I want you to have the money. I mean . . . Father, she's like your grandmother too."

Father Britt felt as if he was going to cry. Please don't let me cry, he said to himself. Please don't let me embarrass the boy. A priest who says hell and damn, he can understand and approve of. A priest who cries is something else again.

"I'll tell you what, Rickie. Let's talk about it later. I'll make one more real try at the bishop about the baseball team. This isn't just the time to do it, but first chance I get when I think he might be receptive, I'll put it to him. Straight. And then if it's a question of just the uniforms maybe we can work something out. Meanwhile, get the bike, Rickie. If the bishop says O.K. we could work out some sort of an affair, maybe a carnival or a magic show to raise the money. You could help a lot with that."

"I don't do magic very well, Father."

"I'll teach you. You just happen to be talking to the best magician in the Archdiocese of New York."

"No kidding?"

"Would I kid you, Rickie?"

"No, Father. I didn't mean it that way. You really do tricks? Magic?"

"Magic, Rickie."

170

"Gee."

"Just one thing more, Rickie, before you go."

"Yes, Father?"

"Would you tell me something? On the square? Not because I'm your priest but because I have to know. Because it's very important to me?"

"Sure, Father."

"You really did see the Lady?"

"I swear it, Father."

"It's not just some kind of a joke, Rickie? I won't be mad if it was. Not if you tell me now."

"Gee, Father Britt, I wouldn't do anything like that. I seen the Lady. I swear it. I swear it on my mother's grave."

"Your mother's still very much alive, Rickie."

"I know. But she's got a grave. Over in Calvary. New Calvary."

"You swear before God, Rickie. Think of that carefully now. I'm talking to you now as a priest. And when you talk to a priest, Rickie, like you do in confession, you're not just talking to a priest, you're talking to God. Directly to God. You swear to God, Rickie, you did see her?"

The boy crossed himself and raised his right hand and put his left over his heart. "I swear to God. I seen the Lady."

The priest put his arm around the boy's shoulder and rumpled his hair. "I thought so, Rickie. I really thought so."

"I wouldn't lie about that. Not about that, Father."

"I didn't think you would."

"You'll remember about the uniforms? Mom won't be giving me the money until my birthday. That's not for a month and a half yet . . . so if you change your mind, let me know."

171

"I will, Rickie."

"I mean, it isn't like I was doing you a big favor or something. I mean, some of it should go back to the church. I mean, *She* wouldn't pick just any church, would She? She picked St. Martin's."

"There's something to that."

"Can I come and see you again? Maybe you'd teach me how to handicap horses. Mom says you're better than Ken Kling or the *Green Sheet*."

"There have been worse things put on tombstones, Rickie."

"Sure, Father," said the boy, not quite sure what the priest meant.

"Come and see me anytime, Rickie, and keep your arm in shape. One good pitcher is worth ten showy short stops."

Dinner was early that night. It was always early on Monday nights as a courtesy to Father Kincaid and his Ladies' Sodality Church history class. He liked a good two-hour practice in front of the mirror before exposing himself on the lecture platform to the fifty-three women enrolled in the class. Father Kincaid believed in leaving nothing to chance, inspiration or the spur of the moment. He rehearsed his lecture, his gestures and his silences. "Silence," he once told Father Britt, "is the lecturer's most important weapon. A judicious pause adds weight to what the speaker has said and gives the slow-witted members of the audience a chance to catch up."

The lemon meringue pie was a huge success and Father Britt paid Mrs. Doody the ultimate compliment. He had two slices and a sliver along with four cups of her very good, very hot coffee. While he was still finishing the fourth cup

172

of coffee, Father Kincaid excused himself from the table and went to his room to prepare himself for the Ladies' Sodality. Mrs. Doody brought her cup of coffee to the table and sat with Father Britt.

"A wonderful meal, Mrs. Doody."

"Thank you, Father."

"And that lemon meringue pie! Wonderful!"

"Do you mind if I poke my nose into your business a little, Father?"

"Poke ahead, Mrs. Doody. After that meal I can't deny you anything."

"Willie Brandt brought you another one of those pictures, didn't he?"

"Did he tell you that?"

"Not right out, he didn't. From some of the things he said and from a good look I had at what he was carrying when he came in, I guessed. He did, didn't he?"

"You guessed right, Mrs. Doody."

"It was crying?"

Father Britt nodded. "Mrs. Fuller had one, too. The bishop's had ten and the newspapers have another ten or fifteen. There's an epidemic of crying pictures, Mrs. Doody."

Mrs. Doody crossed herself. "Sometimes, Father," she said, "I don't think the good Lord shows much confidence in us."

"What do you mean by that?"

"The pictures, Father. Why so many? Isn't one miracle enough? Or was He afraid we wouldn't get the idea with just one? He has to flood us with them."

"Looking at it that way it does show a certain lack of faith in our understanding, doesn't it?"

173

"The Lord works in mysterious ways, Father."

"He does indeed, Mrs. Doody."

"Sometimes I think you're too hard on him."

"The Lord?"

"Father Kincaid. I know how he gets on your nerves sometimes. I shouldn't be saying this, should I? I shouldn't be talking about a priest that way."

"Come on, Mrs. Doody. We know each other too well for you to pretend to be humble."

"He *does* get on your nerves. I've seen it. He's young, Father, and insecure. But I think he does have the Vocation for it. And you did jump on him about the vestments."

"Vestments! If he has, as you suggest, the Vocation, it's about time he learned the hard facts of living with a bishop. He really thinks the bishop would allow us to take some of that collection money and spend it on new vestments . . . he really does."

"He likes you very much, Father. I've seen that too."

"Mrs. Doody . . . don't kid a kidder."

"He thinks you're old-fashioned and set in your ways but he respects you and likes you. Is it so wrong that a young priest should also be in awe of his bishop and want to make a good impression on him . . . and take his side when there is a dispute? Is that so wrong or so unnatural, Father?"

"No. I did it myself, I'm sure."

"Be patient with him. He's a good boy. He wants to reform the church . . . and you . . . and probably me. He says a good Mass, Father."

"He does. A little glib for my taste . . . a little rolling it around in his mouth . . . but a good Mass."

174

"Be patient with him, Father. He's not as sure of himself as we sometimes think he is."

"All right, Mrs. Doody. As a gesture of appreciation for your coffee and your lemon meringue pie I'll be patient with him. Anything else on your mind?"

"I'm just passing the time of the day with you, Father. I hope you don't think . . ."

"Mrs. Doody, don't kid a kidder. What's on your social calendar tonight? A visit to the recreation hall for the Ladies' Sodality Church history class?"

"Them! The movies, father. I'm getting too old to make up my own dreams. The movies do it fine for me."

"Mrs. Doody, may I ask you a personal question? How old are you?"

"Old enough to know better. Over twenty-one, Father. That's all the government of the United States has to know to let me vote. Over twenty-one, Father."

"About as much over twenty-one as I am."

"Just about, Father. Give or take a couple of years."

"Are you happy here? We sometimes take you for granted. Is there anything we should be doing for you that we don't do?"

"Not a blessed thing, Father. Not a blessed thing. I have my room, my radio, my kitchen and the two of you to look after. What else would I need? You already did the big thing for me, Father!"

"What was that, Mrs. Doody?"

"Getting the bishop to allow me to live in the rectory. Before that, when I was just here to clean up and cook the meals and then go home to my room, it was like I was a servant. Now I'm part of St. Martin's. Like you and Father

175

Kincaid. I belong somewhere. This is my home, Father. And it's a good home."

"I'm glad you feel that way, Mrs. Doody."

"I do, Father. I really do. And what will you be doing with yourself tonight?"

"I'll read a little and watch the bishop's television program."

Mrs. Doody smiled.

"You make it sound like penance, Father."

"I do, don't I?"

"Why don't you get out of the rectory, Father? Take a walk, go see Herman Wekstein . . . go to a movie."

"I might at that. I have a hunch that Herman will be around later. He's worried about me. You may run into Sarah at the movie. When Herman gets worried about me he packs Sarah off to the movie and thinks up an excuse to drop by the rectory."

"It's a science-fiction picture tonight, Father."

"I sometimes think that's a contradiction of terms."

"What's that, Father?"

"Nothing, Mrs. Doody. Have a good time at the movie."

Father Britt finished his coffee, and went into his study but, instead of reading, sat back in his chair with his eyes closed. He'd been there almost an hour when he heard the bell ring. He sat still, expecting Mrs. Doody to answer it. Then realizing that she was probably at the local movie house, he got to his feet and went to the door and opened it.

Herman Wekstein was standing on the top step, grinning.

"I was expecting you," said Father Britt.

"You were? Who said anything about coming?"

"Nobody. I was just expecting you."

176

"A man has a wife can't live without seeing a science-fiction movie, he should sit home alone?"

"You told me Sarah couldn't stand science-fiction pictures. You said they confused her."

"She's learning. Can I come in?"

"I'm sorry, Herman, come in."

"I'm not disturbing you? You're not doing anything?"

"What would I be doing?"

"Collecting tears from pictures? How did the hypodermic needle work?"

Father Britt said nothing. He led Herman into his study, sat back in his chair. Herman took the chair beside the desk and put a package on the desk.

"What's that?" asked the priest.

"Bourbon," said Herman. "So, I felt like having a drink. I brought my own. I don't trust the quality of your cellar, Maurie."

The priest went out into the kitchen and came back with two glasses and a pitcher of water.

"Forgive my ignorance," he said. "I didn't know whether you take water with bourbon."

"Branch water they call it."

"You'll settle for tap water?" asked Father Britt.

"Settle for it? I prefer it."

He opened the bottle of bourbon and poured a glass half full, adding water to fill it to the brim. He looked at the priest, holding the bottle tilted over the second glass.

"Bourbon, Maurie? Or is it against your religion?"

"A medicinal snort."

Herman passed the glass across to the priest after putting an inch of bourbon in the glass and filling the rest up with water. They raised their glasses, saluted and drank.

Father Britt coughed and took another pull at his glass. "Very good," he said.

"How would a decent Catholic priest know the relative merits of bourbon?"

"It must be good, Herman. It burns . . . all the way down."

"A good rule of thumb, Maurie. We'll make a drinker out of you yet."

"You may at that, Herman."

"How are you, Maurie?"

"Fine, Herman. Fine."

"Are you?"

"Why wouldn't I be?"

"You're right, Maurie. Why wouldn't you be?"

They drank in silence.

"How many crying pictures do you have now, Maurie?"

"Four. Who told you there were others?"

"Willie Brandt, for one. He came in the store this afternoon. He told me about the picture he found."

"I made him promise not to say anything to anybody about it."

"He had some sober second thoughts after turning it over to you. He's afraid he might get into trouble with the bishop. Don't ask me why or how. It's just something he has in his mind. He also, I'm afraid, is beginning to think he let his heart overrule his head."

"What does that mean?"

"He's wondering if maybe the picture has some monetary value. He's wondering if he might have been better off calling a newspaper instead of handing it over to his priest. The lesson of the by-line story by Rickie Prosser wasn't lost on him."

"Herman, I'll tell you the truth. I'll be happy to give it back to him. At this moment, the Archdiocese of New York is loaded with crying pictures."

"More of them?"

"According to the bishop, there are twenty-five or thirty of them at last count."

"That's going to raise hell with the miracle market. Probably knock the bottom right out of it."

"It's not funny, Herman."

"I find it rather amusing, Maurie."

"Well, I don't."

"Hold on now. Maurie, come on. This is Herman Wekstein . . . the friendly corner druggist. Don't get your back up at me."

"I'm sorry, Herman."

The priest got up and poured two more drinks. He made his stronger, and Herman's weaker.

"Shouldn't we put some ice cubes in it?" he asked.

"Serious bourbon drinkers frown on ice cubes," said Herman.

"Let's," said the priest, "be serious by all means."

"What is the matter, Maurie? The pictures? The bishop? The pains in your chest?"

"None of them. Or all of them. You really want me to tell you, Herman?"

"Why not? I don't guarantee absolution the way you do but I'm dispensing the same medicine you dispense in that wooden box of yours . . . an ear to listen to you."

Father Britt finished the drink and went to the bottle and

179

poured himself another one. He looked questioningly at the druggist who took the hint, swallowed his drink and passed over the empty glass, which the priest filled.

"Do you think you should have another one, Maurie? You're not used to it."

"Don't worry about me acquiring a bad habit, Herman. By the time it got to be a habit I'd be dead. That's one of the minor virtues of old age."

"Oh . . . it's to be one of those nights."

"Why not? Is the priest to be denied self-pity once in a while. You have no idea how much self-pity I've listened to since I got out of the seminary."

"That's your job, Maurie. Don't come complaining to me about your working conditions."

"No, I suppose that's what I'm doing."

"What *is* wrong?"

"Will you allow me a certain amount of self-pity?"

"Sure, Maurie. A certain amount."

"I had a pain in my chest today. I felt dizzy . . ."

"I told you, Maurie, you shouldn't . . ."

"Don't interrupt me."

Both men were startled by the vehemence of Father Britt's answer. They stared at each other for a minute. The priest smiled, nodded his head twice and said, "I'm sorry, Herman. If I'm to have my fair share of self-pity you must let me tell you about it in my own way."

"Go ahead, Maurie."

"I was suddenly afraid, Herman. Afraid of death."

"Why should you be immune?"

"That's the point. I *should* be. I'm a priest. What is death to me? It's an incident in the march from one eternity to another. Have you ever been to a priest's funeral, Herman? It's not like any funeral you've ever been to. There isn't any weeping or wailing. He is eulogized and his works are remembered and talked about, but to the other priests present he is moving on to his reward. Don't smirk, Herman. We believe that. His *reward*. Don't you think when a priest gets to be my age he looks forward to his death sometimes? Don't you think once in a while he cries, 'Enough, Father. Enough. I am ready for the next step. I want to see Thy face and know the comfort of Thy staff'?"

"I suppose so."

"Death, to a priest . . . a good priest, Herman . . . death is nothing to fear or be apprehensive about. And yet today . . . the thought of death terrified me."

"And what inference are you trying to draw from that? That you aren't a good priest? That it shows weakness? Maurie, you are also a man. And once in a while is it too terrible if the man takes precedence over the priest?"

"Yes. It is. Terrible. I am a priest or I'm nothing."

"Are you telling me, Maurie, that you've never had any doubts?"

"Doubts are for the seminary student. Doubts! Merciful Father, could I have doubts at my age? Is that possible? Because, I tell you, Herman, if it *is* possible I've more than wasted my life . . . I've profaned it."

The druggist leaned back in the chair, put his feet up on the priest's desk and lit a cigar. He puffed on it, and gave his full attention to the priest.

"Profaned it," repeated the priest. "I've believed in the Church. In the Doctrine. In the Faith. In the Truth. If I find now that I don't really believe . . . think for a moment of what I might have had out of my life. I might have had a family and children. I won't tell you the number of hours I've spent on my knees before God asking forgiveness because in my heart I wanted a son. A family. If now, at the end of my life I don't believe, look what I've sacrificed for something that doesn't matter."

"And you worry that you don't believe, Maurie, because this afternoon you felt a sudden cold chill down the back of your neck at the idea of death. How many times do you think I've felt that cold chill? You've felt it only once. Hardly a week goes by that I don't feel it. Sometimes it comes when I'm reading the obituary pages of the newspaper and noticing the ages of the newly deceased. Sometimes I can't sleep at night and I listen to my heart pounding and feel a quiver that could be the beginning of a coronary. I've lived with that cold chill for the past twenty-five years, Maurie. And you feel it once and begin to doubt your Vocation and the way you've spent your life."

"But you're not a priest, Herman."

"I'm something even more committed than that. I'm a man who doesn't believe in anything. Or rather, I believe that the end is the end . . . that death means extinction. This is it . . . and when it's over, it's over. There's nothing else. Unless you want to split hairs and call oblivion something. If I really believe in the oblivion of death . . . why should I get the chills down my back?"

"Because if you really do believe in nothing . . . you would want to put off facing that nothingness as long as possible."

"You have a point, Maurie."

"You really don't believe in anything, Herman? There

are no nagging doubts in the back of your mind?"

"No nagging doubts, Maurie. But there is one similarity between us. I'm no surer of my lack of belief than you are about your faith. You have one big advantage over me. If you're right, you'll know it. If I'm right, I won't."

"No religion at all, Herman?"

"None. I won't accept your pious vagueness . . . purgatory . . . hell . . . heaven. Where are they? What do they look like? Do they have indoor plumbing? I'll tell you something, Maurie, since this seems to be the night to purge ourselves. Do you think I started out to be a druggist? I wanted to be a doctor. From the time I was old enough to know anything I wanted to be a doctor. I didn't make it. I flunked out. So I settled for the next best thing. You know the only religion that would have a chance with me? Reincarnation. Now there's a carefully spelled-out belief. The religion of the second chance. So I didn't make it as a doctor this time. Fine . . . next time I'm born I'll take another crack at it. And if I don't make it that time, I'll try again. With eternity to fool around in, I'm bound to make it sooner or later. There's a religion with real popular appeal. Nobody can be a loser forever. So you're a hunchback or have only one eye . . . put up with it for sixty years. Next time around we'll give you all the equipment."

"You're serious about this, Herman?"

"Half serious, anyway."

"You don't know the first thing about what it's like to be a priest."

"How could I?"

"First of all, the mere fact that you feel you have the Call sets you aside from the rest of the world."

183

"Isn't there a kind of arrogance in that, Maurie? To think that of all the young men in the world you are one of the elect who've been chosen. Doesn't the very word you use, 'call,' have a kind of built-in vanity to it?"

"I suppose it might seem that way to you."

"It does, Maurie. It certainly does."

"All right. I thought I had the Call. All during my years in the seminary I examined myself to find out if I really was suited to the life of a priest. I searched my soul and my conscience to find out if I was truly a man of God. Literally a man of God, Herman. Not a priest or a seminary student. A man of God."

"And you convinced yourself."

"No. I never convinced myself. But my doubts weren't strong enough to drive me back into the temporal world. Even a seminary student has to give God the benefit of the doubt. So I was ordained and became a priest. I don't know whether the words will mean anything to you, Herman, but there were moments of ecstasy and revelation. They sound cheap and commonplace, those two words, but they're not. Ecstasy during a Mass . . . now and then, when suddenly I felt very close to God. Revelation when God revealed himself to me . . . ."

"Like the Lady did to Rickie Prosser."

Father Britt slammed his fist down on the table. "You shouldn't scoff, Herman. You shouldn't! If you haven't any respect for my religion, I insist that you respect me as a friend. You'll listen, but you must not scoff."

"I'm sorry, Maurie. I told you I couldn't give you absolution."

"Do you know what the word 'revelation' means when a

priest uses it? You either do or you don't and if you don't I have no words to explain it to you. 'God reveals,' is the closest I can come to it. Reveals. Revelation. All through my early years as a priest, Herman, I questioned and doubted. Not my God or my religion. Myself. My worthiness to be a priest. My Vocation. My Call. I even wanted what Rickie Prosser got . . . a vision . . . an old-fashioned vision. I wanted to see the heavens open up and a figure come out of a blinding ray of light and say . . . 'Maurie Britt, you are one of the chosen ones.' I felt I was dealing with my God secondhand. I wanted a close-up look, a personal relationship. You know something, Herman?"

"What?"

"Pride and vanity are sins even for my parishioners. Can you imagine how much deadlier sins they are to a priest? And what was it after all but sin and pride for me to want God to reassure me personally?"

"That's what you told yourself at the seminary?"

"That's what I've told myself all my life. I was reconciled to having a secondhand, once-removed relationship with God . . . I didn't believe or worship any the less because of it. If anything, I was disappointed that I wasn't worthy enough for something more."

"And then the picture on your wall began to cry."

"You knew I was coming to that?"

"Of course you were coming to that, Maurie. Didn't your crying picture give some of the rest of us something to think about? It didn't convert me. It just added another small doubt to an already doubting nonbelief."

"Before the picture there was Rickie Prosser and his vision. You know what unbidden thought came into my head when he ran in and told me about it?"

"Another doubt?"

"No. Not for a minute. Not for a minute did I doubt that he'd seen it. You know what went through my mind? How unfair it was for Our Lady to reveal Herself to an eleven-year-old boy who wrote dirty words on a tenement hallway . . . and as she had revealed Herself to peasant children in Portugal . . . or to a young girl in France . . . and not to a devout servant who had served faithfully and was desperately in need of reassurance at the end of his life. Just for a second, Herman, but the thought was there. Then it happened."

"The picture."

"My miracle, Herman. Mine! A miracle . . . for Maurie Britt. The thing I'd waited for all my life. The firsthand contact. The acknowledgment of my existence and my need. The picture cried. *My* picture. An instant after I had sent that flush of anger up to heaven as a cry for help."

"I never considered that you would feel that way about it."

"Why should you? Herman, I know what you think of me—a pleasant, misguided man. You feel great friendship and compassion for me."

"I never thought you were misguided, Maurie. But I didn't think you believed Rickie."

"Of course I believed him."

"In your years as a priest you must have come across other people who have seen visions. My psychiatrist friends tell me it's a common delusion in a particular kind of mental illness."

"Nonsense. I believe in the Blessed Sacrament even though a scientific analysis of the Host before and after consecra-

186

tion would show no difference. Just as I'd have believed the tears on my picture if *only I* had seen them and there was no evidence that they'd ever existed, except in my consciousness."

"You believe what you want to believe."

"In the case of the picture, Herman, I don't have to answer that statement. I saw the tears. You saw the tears. Mrs. Prosser saw the tears. They existed. It was my miracle. It was what I'd been praying for all my life. It was the final revelation and . . . I know the word makes you uncomfortable . . . my ecstasy. And then what happened? What happened, Herman? What happened to my miracle?" Father Britt poured himself another drink.

"Take it easy on the bourbon, Maurie," said Herman.

The old priest sat down at his desk with the glass of bourbon in his hand. He looked at it . . . held it up toward the light and stared at it in fascination. His eyes were dull and glazed. With some astonishment, Herman Wekstein realized that the old priest was very drunk.

Father Britt put the glass of bourbon down on the desk and looked at his friend. "What happened to my miracle, Herman? *My* miracle! It became the bishop's miracle, Mrs. Fuller's miracle, Willie Brandt's miracle . . . the miracle of the ten people who sent pictures to the bishop . . . the miracle of the twenty other people who sent pictures to the newspapers. That's what happened to my miracle. And I sit and feel the cold wind of death on the back of my neck again . . . still on my knees . . . still trying to make contact with my God . . . As unsure and rejected . . . as I was way back in the seminary."

"Take it easy, Maurie . . ."

"Or what? Or you'll tell the bishop? And what does the bishop say about my miracle? Nothing until he asks his public-relations man what to say. Herman, was there a public-relations man at the Last Supper? And which of the disciples told Jesus whether to ride the raft or sink it? And which of us is better off? You believe in nothing so you are never disappointed. I believe in everything . . ."

Father Britt started to cry and Herman Wekstein got up from his chair and went to him . . .

"I feel sick, Herman," said the priest. "I feel sick."

The druggist put his arm around his shoulder and for a second held the head of the priest against his chest. "Come on, Maurie. I'll help you up to bed."

Father Britt got to his feet. "I'll make it on my own, Herman. Am I drunk? Is that what it is?"

"You put away a lot of good bourbon."

"I never used the hypodermic needle, Herman. Are miracles something you send to a testing laboratory? I think I'll lie down. Forgive me, Herman. I *do* feel sick. Good-night."

Father Britt walked out of the den. Herman Wekstein debated going with him and helping him into bed but decided against it. He'll feel bad enough in the morning, he reasoned. There was no necessity of adding that final indignity to Father Britt's memory of the evening.

Herman took the priest's glass out to the kitchen and washed it thoroughly before putting it back in the cupboard. Then he came back into the den and picked up his own glass and the rest of the bottle of bourbon and carried it into the rectory parlor. He settled himself in an old-fashioned Morris chair, poured himself a straight shot of bourbon, put his feet up and reached over and turned on the television set. While he waited for it to warm up he took a sip, got up and stood in the hallway and listened. He thought he heard a noise upstairs so he went up to Father Britt's room. The priest was asleep. Herman Wekstein looked down at him for a moment and then carefully covered him with a blanket. He picked up the priest's clothes, which had been dropped carelessly on the floor, folded the trousers at the crease and hung them on a hanger. He put the socks and shirt in the clothes hamper in the bathroom, and hung up the coat.

"I never thought he'd wear a nightshirt," he said to himself and began to giggle. At the sound, Father Britt turned in bed restlessly and Herman tiptoed out of the room, closing the door noiselessly behind him.

"A nightshirt," he repeated as he went down the stairs. When he returned to the parlor he sat down and watched a Western.

He thought of leaving but decided to stay until Mrs. Doody returned from the movies. He knew Sarah wouldn't be home before then and for a peculiar reason that he did not quite understand he did not want to go home to an empty house tonight or leave the priest alone. He wondered when Father Kincaid would return. The upsurge of music told him that the Western was ending so he switched channels and turned to another Western that was just beginning. Midway in the program the bell rang. Herman paid no attention to it until it rang for the third time. Then he got to his feet, turned off the TV set, capped the bottle of bourbon, placed it under his chair and went to the door.

The man standing on the steps was wearing a derby and a chesterfield. As Herman Wekstein opened the door, he swept the derby off his head and held it in front of his chest.

"Good evening," he said.

"Good evening," said Herman.

"Is Father Britt in?"

"Yes, he is."

"May I see him?"

"No," said Herman.

"I beg your pardon?" said the man.

"I said no. You can't see Father Britt."

"Oh," said the man. He put his derby back on his head and turned to go. He took two steps and turned again.

"Why?" he asked.

"Why?"

"Why can't I see Father Britt?"

"He isn't feeling well. He's in bed."

"A virus?"

"No."

"A cold?"

"No."

"A headache?"

"No."

"Oh," said the man, preparing to leave again.

"Why don't you come and see him tomorrow. He'll be much better then," said Herman.

"I'd like to see him tonight."

"I'm afraid you can't."

"Oh," said the man.

He took two steps forward, removed the derby again.

"Are you connected with St. Martin's?" he asked.

"Only socially," said Herman.

"Oh," said the man.

190

"I'm a friend of Father Britt," said Herman. "You might say I'm Father Britt's spiritual adviser."

"Oh," said the man with the derby held across his chest. "And would you mind telling me your name?"

"Wekstein. Herman Wekstein."

"Wekstein?" asked the man. "This is the rectory of St. Martin's, isn't it?"

"Come in," said Herman.

"Thank you."

Herman led the man into the parlor of the rectory, took his hat and coat and put it on the chair, motioned the visitor into the Morris chair, sat himself down in the chair next to the table and looked at the guest expectantly. The latter reached into the inside pocket of his coat and took out a wallet. He extracted a card from the wallet and passed it over to Herman.

Herman read it. "Dan Gross. Religious Objects, Prayer Books. Statuary."

"The word 'statuary' is something of an exaggeration," said Mr. Gross. "What it actually means are those little plastic figures you may have seen on the dashboards of cars."

"I've seen them," said Herman.

"They've caught on amazingly well. They actually outsell those large felt dice that people like to hang from the rear-view mirror for luck. A much classier item."

"I suppose so," said Herman.

"Are you sure I can't see Father Britt?"

"Quite sure."

"And is it all right to talk to you?"

"All right with whom?" asked Herman.

191

"With anybody. I mean, Father Britt is the one I should see."

"Anything you have to tell Father Britt, you can tell me, Mr. Gross. Father Britt and I are very close friends and I'll be happy to tell him about your visit and warn him to expect a call from you tomorrow."

"Wekstein? Is that what you said your name was?"

"Wekstein."

"There aren't many, are there?"

"Many what?"

"Jewish converts. Forgive me for prying, Mr. Wekstein, but it is unusual."

"I suppose it is. Would you like a shot of bourbon, Mr. Gross?"

"Bourbon? Here?"

"Would you or wouldn't you?"

"That would be very hospitable," said Mr. Gross.

"Fine," said Herman.

He got to his feet and reached between Mr. Gross's legs and pulled the bottle of bourbon out from under the chair.

Mr. Gross smiled tentatively.

"Be right back," said Herman. "Don't move."

"I won't," said Mr. Gross.

Herman got a second glass out of the cupboard . . . went into the den to get the pitcher of water and returned to the parlor and poured two drinks. "Water?" he asked.

"Please," said Mr. Gross.

Herman poured water in the second glass. He mixed himself a drink too . . . mainly bourbon and sat back. "What can I do for you, Mr. Gross?"

"Oh, I'm already a Catholic, Mr. Wekstein. It would be

192

peculiar if I wasn't, considering my line of work, wouldn't it?"

"Religious objects. Prayer books. Statuary."

"This is the St. Martin's and the Father Britt that was in all the papers? The crying picture?"

"This is it."

"I wanted to make sure. That's what I wanted to see Father Britt about. The crying picture."

"Mr. Gross, I think I know why you're here."

"You do?"

"About the crying picture? Right?"

"Right? I said so. Or at least I inferred it."

"You have another one."

"One!" said Mr. Gross. "One?"

He reached into his pocket and extracted a piece of paper from his wallet.

"One!" he said. "I have fifteen hundred and forty-three."

"Fifteen hundred and forty-three?"

"A warehouse full of them, Mr. Wekstein. That's why I wanted to see Father Britt. I wanted to tell him the facts in the case before he made a fool of himself about his miracle."

"Please explain yourself, Mr. Gross."

"They're my pictures. I manufacture them. I sell them to the retail outlets . . . the stores that deal in religious supplies, Mr. Wekstein. When I first read about the crying picture here in the rectory of St. Martin's I knew it must have been one of mine. So I checked. I discovered that Father Britt bought the picture in a store just five blocks away on the Avenue. I don't know whether you've been listening to the radio tonight, Mr. Wekstein, but there are now about fifty crying pictures. So far nobody has put two and two

193

together and discovered the one thing all these pictures have in common."

"And what's that, Mr. Gross?"

"They were all manufactured by me. All part of the same shipment that went out to the retail stores in 1942. Does that suggest anything to you?"

"Go on, Mr. Gross."

"In 1942, Mr. Wekstein. The middle of the war. Do you remember what it was like during the war? Rationing. Supplies difficult to get. Synthetics in strategic materials. Remember? That particular picture was one of my best items. Always sold well. It was a quality item. Printed on good stock paper, excellent colors, quality inks. Over the course of the past thirty years I've sold perhaps a hundred thousand copies of the picture. All of them were first-rate quality. Except, Mr. Wekstein, except that one shipment . . . in the middle of the war. It was difficult to get the kind of paper I'd been using. The inks used then were of an inferior quality, but there was a continuing demand for the picture and I ran off this one batch . . . twenty-five hundred copies. I, of course, adjusted the price accordingly. This business, perhaps more than any other is based on public faith . . . a fair product at a fair price. It would have been ridiculous for me to pretend that this particular run was on a quality par with the others. I told the retailers the truth and cut the price accordingly."

"Just a minute, Mr. Gross," said Herman.

He went out into the hall and listened. There was no sound from the upper floor. When he came back into the parlor he carefully closed the door behind him.

"Go ahead, Mr. Gross, please."

194

"They started coming back about two years later. There wasn't a week, Mr. Wekstein, when one or two of them didn't come back. By that time, we were able to get better material and in each case I replaced the one that was returned with a new one. All the faith in this business isn't on one side, Mr. Wekstein. I have an obligation to show good faith too. Good faith . . . good business . . . if you know what I mean."

"Why were they returned, Mr. Gross?"

"Because the inks ran. In some cases the paper buckled. In others, moisture developed on the picture. I wasn't surprised. I expected it, more or less. You understand I turned out that batch of inferior pictures only because I was being pressured by the retailers. I explained to them the circumstances but they didn't seem to mind and so I supplied them. In any line of work, Mr. Wekstein, you have to satisfy your retailers or you're in serious trouble."

"Until the other day, Mr. Gross, nobody ascribed supernatural motives to the moisture or the smudges?"

"Of course not. Frankly, Mr. Wekstein, I can't understand what all the excitement is about. I haven't seen Father Britt's picture but I've seen more than fifteen hundred like it and quite honestly it would never occur to me to suspect anything but what happened . . . inferior material . . . inferior ink and inferior paper. As I said, I have had more than fifteen hundred returned to me. There must be another eight or nine hundred floating around and judging by past performances they have, or are about to start crying."

"Why did you come to Father Britt, Mr. Gross?"

"To try to convince him that this isn't a miracle. It's one of those unfortunate by-products of a wartime shortage.

Frankly, Mr. Wekstein, I'm in a business that is dependent on the good will and confidence of the Church. The last thing in the world I can afford to do is get involved in a fight with a bishop. And if Father Britt insists on calling it a miracle when the bishop says it isn't . . . sooner or later somebody is going to discover the real reason those pictures were crying and I'll be out of business. Bishops don't like to be made fools of, Mr. Wekstein, and that's what the bishop will think has happened to him when the story gets out."

Herman Wekstein got to his feet and poured two more drinks.

"Thank you," said Mr. Gross, "don't mind if I do."

"Mr. Gross," said Herman, "who else have you told this to?"

"Nobody. I intended telling it to nobody but Father Britt. I told it to you because you are a close friend of Father Britt's . . . because your name is Wekstein and because somebody has to tell Father Britt to shut up about his miracle before the whole thing explodes in all our faces."

"You have no intention of going to the newspapers with this story?"

"Are you crazy? Forgive me, Mr. Wekstein, I didn't mean to be that vehement. Going to the newspapers would be the last thing I'd do. Do you think any manufacturer wants the newspapers to know he made an inferior product? Even under difficult wartime conditions? Even under pressure from his retailers? Going to the newspapers would be the last thing I'd do."

"Or the bishop?"

"Have you met the bishop, Mr. Wekstein?"

"I've had that pleasure."

196

"Then that should answer your question. All I want is for the whole thing to blow over. But it won't if your Father Britt keeps screaming that it's a miracle. That will only get the bishop's back up and he'll start checking into those particular pictures."

"Don't you think sooner or later some newspaper reporter is going to get curious and start checking?"

"Sooner or later. If the story stays alive."

"You said yourself the radio was full of the story tonight. It's a fair guess the papers will be tomorrow. What makes you think the story will die soon?"

"It'll die soon if no more crying pictures turn up and if Father Britt stops talking about miracles and turning it into a debate with a bishop. I've already contacted some of the stores that stocked that particular run of pictures and replaced those I've found. There are other stores that still have them in stock. I'll find those and replace them. I just want Father Britt to keep quiet about a miracle. If the story gets out we'll both look bad."

"Excuse me just a minute, Mr. Gross," said Herman. "I'll be right back. Help yourself to some more of the bourbon while I'm gone."

"Don't mind if I do," said Mr. Gross.

Herman returned in a few minutes carrying the picture Willie Brandt had given to Father Britt earlier that day. He had assumed Father Britt kept it in the den and found it almost immediately on the top of the closet. He handed it to Dan Gross.

Gross took it . . . held it in his lap, looked at it from a distance and then reached into his pocket, took out a pair of glasses and put them on. He studied the picture, held it up to the light, turned it around and finally turned it over.

"This is one of them," he said.

"How can you be so sure?"

"Look here. Look at the ink around the eyes. See how it's smudged. Now here," he turned the picture over, "see this little number in the lower right-hand corner?"

Herman looked and saw an almost microscopic "16" in the corner.

"That's the code number for that shipment. Believe me, Mr. Wekstein, I've seen it often enough to know it without looking it up. This is one of them."

"How do you explain the fact that suddenly twenty or thirty of them started crying . . . to use the newspaper phrase . . . now? Why now . . . in the last day or two?"

"It's happened all the time since they were put in the retail stores, Mr. Wekstein. Nobody ever thought anything about them except that they'd been stung with a bad job of printing. But now, suddenly your Father Britt is all over the front pages saying it's a miracle. Everybody that's been stung . . . that's their thought, Mr. Wekstein, not mine . . . You can't say anybody is stung when I'm willing to make good and replace the picture. Anyway . . . all of a sudden they're all thinking they have something special. A crying picture. A miracle. Without your Father Britt making such a big thing of it, I'd have been able to get back all twenty-five hundred of them eventually without anybody being any the wiser and without jeopardizing my good business relationship with the Catholic Church."

"There won't be any more talk about a miracle."

"I'm not doubting you, Mr. Wekstein. But I'd rather hear that from Father Britt himself."

"Please don't."

"I don't understand you. Please don't what?"

"Please don't call him. Please don't tell him."

"If I don't tell him, he'll just keep the whole thing alive. Even a Catholic priest who insists on seeing a miracle must have to face up to the facts once he knows them."

"You don't understand, Mr. Gross."

"You're the one who doesn't understand, Mr. Wekstein. If I am connected with these pictures it could ruin my business. The Catholic Church is a tight-knit organization. All it would take would be for the word to go out from somebody in authority . . . somebody like Bishop O'Leary . . . not to deal with Dan Gross anymore and I'd be out of business."

"You said yourself that the bishop could connect you with the pictures . . . or a newspaper reporter."

"Nobody is going to bother if the story dies. And the story will die if Father Britt doesn't keep it alive by continuing to call it a miracle."

"I promise you he'll say nothing more about it being a miracle."

"I need more than your promise. Mr. Wekstein, let's understand each other. Don't think that because of the nature of the product I deal in I'm any less ruthless than any other businessman would be when his livelihood is threatened. There is no way I can be traced to these crying pictures."

"What about the code number you just showed me?"

"The '16'? Yes, they were on the back of each of the pictures in that unfortunate run. You know what I've been doing for the past two days? I've been running off more copies of that picture . . . on good paper . . . with good ink and on the back of each of them I put the number '16.' By tomorrow I will have replaced the stock in every retail store that buys these pictures from me . . . in place of the copies they have on hand I will have given them the new copies . . . and all of them will have the code number on the back. So nobody will be able to tell which lot was made when. Nobody can verify the story I told you . . . but I want to see Father Britt and tell it to him because when I do he'll stop talking about miracles and the whole thing will die. That's what I want."

"I give you my promise that he will make no more statements about miracles. Isn't that enough?"

"I'd want to hear that from him."

"I won't let you," said Herman Wekstein. "I won't let you. Do you hear me? I won't let you."

He got to his feet and grabbed Dan Gross by the shirt front and pulled him out of the chair. He held him firmly. "I won't let you."

Gross tried to pull himself free and the two men wrestled around the parlor. Herman Wekstein, the sweat pouring off his face, pushed Gross against the wall and held him there. Gross's face was red and the veins in his neck stood out. There was fear in his eyes and he tried frantically to loosen the druggist's grip.

"You won't. You won't," screamed Herman. "I won't let you . . ."

He was suddenly gripped from behind and his hands were wrenched from around Gross's shirt front. Father Kincaid lifted him firmly, but gently, and deposited him in the chair. Herman sat panting and slowly put his hands over his face.

200

Dan Gross moved across the room and grabbed his hat and coat and started toward the door. Father Kincaid stopped him.

"Just a minute," he said. "Just a minute. Mr. Wekstein would you like to tell me what this is all about?"

Dan Gross extracted a card from his wallet. He handed it to Father Kincaid.

"Are you Father Britt?" he asked.

"No, I'm Father Kincaid. Now what's going on?"

"Ask him," said Herman Wekstein. His face was still buried in his hands.

"Well, Mr. Gross?"

"I have nothing to say, Father."

"We'll have none of that. I demand an explanation and I intend to have one."

Herman Wekstein raised his head. "Put your muscles away, Father. I'll tell you," he said. "Can I offer anyone a drink?"

Father Kincaid noticed the bottle of bourbon for the first time. He went over to it, lifted it, held it up to the light and put it down on the table.

"Was that full, Mr. Wekstein?"

"Father, that has nothing to do with it."

"Doesn't it? I come in here and find you in a violent struggle with Mr. Gross. I find a bourbon bottle on the table and you tell me it has nothing to do with it?"

"If you'll stop treating me like an altar boy who's been caught whispering during the service, I'll tell you."

"Suppose you do. And suppose you tell me where Father Britt is."

"Father Britt is upstairs in bed. Asleep."

"And you took advantage of his friendship to use the rectory parlor for a common, drunken brawl."

"Shut up, Father," said Herman Wekstein. "Just shut up and stop talking to your elders in that tone of voice. I am not a member of your Church history class, nor am I a whispering altar boy. Nor am I drunk. Nor was this a brawl. Now just shut up and sit down and listen to me and I'll tell you what it's all about."

Father Kincaid backed away from Herman, reached into his pocket, took out his pipe, filled and lit it. He drew a deep drag on the pipe and expelled the smoke toward the ceiling.

"If I was mistaken, I apologize, Mr. Wekstein. You must admit that from my point of view I had every right to jump to the conclusion I did."

"Mr. Gross, do you want to tell him?" asked Herman.

"I don't want to tell anybody anything. Except Father Britt."

"I am not usually a violent man, Mr. Gross. And I apologize to you for what happened. I haven't been involved in a fight since I was in the third grade. But I tell you this . . . and I mean every word of it. If you tell Father Britt what you told me tonight, I'll kill you. I mean that. I'll kill you."

"Now just a minute," said Father Kincaid. "Just a minute, please. You were going to tell me what it was all about."

"I'll deny everything," said Dan Gross. "Everything. I'll deny it and nobody can prove a thing."

"That'll be enough of that," said Father Kincaid. "All right, Mr. Wekstein. Suppose *you* tell me."

"You tell me something first."

202

"What?"

"How do you feel about Father Britt?"

"What does that have to do with it?"

"Everything, Father Kincaid."

"I respect him as my pastor."

"Nothing more than that?"

"What do you want me to say, Mr. Wekstein?"

"Nothing more than the respect a young priest should have for his pastor? Forget about him as a priest for a moment. How do you feel about him as a man?"

"It would never occur to me to think of him as a man."

"Let it occur to you now, Father Kincaid. Let it occur to you now. We're not playing games. We're talking about a man. We're talking about Maurie Britt. Not Father Britt. Maurie Britt."

"I'm afraid you're not going to get much out of me, Mr. Wekstein, whatever it is you're looking for. All right. He's an old man. He's a good priest but he's an old man. Look, Mr. Wekstein, what do you want? I'm only a couple of years out of a seminary. This is my first parish. Isn't it asking a little too much to expect me to look on my first pastor as a man? He's my pastor. I was terrified of him at first."

"Are you still terrified of him?"

Father Kincaid smiled. "Sometimes. Not as much, or as often. His bark is much worse than his bite. And don't think I don't know what he thinks of me. He thinks I'm faintly ridiculous. He thinks I take myself a little too seriously. He thinks I'm almost completely devoid of humor. Of course I'm faintly ridiculous. Young priests are always faintly ridiculous to old pastors. Of course I take myself seriously. This is a serious Vocation. I'm not Bing Crosby and he's not Barry Fitzgerald. I'm a young priest and he's my pastor. And I'm not completely devoid of humor. Not quite. Not quite, Mr. Wekstein. I read the *New Yorker* every week."

"I accept that as proof."

"Now you're talking to me the way he does. I have no defense against sarcasm. Not even against yours. Now do you want to know some other things? I think his picking winners at the race track is ridiculous and . . . yes, Mr. Wekstein . . . a little shameless. I don't care about the the thing itself. I object, as a Catholic and a priest to his flaunting it. I object to his parishioners accepting it as a rather lovable eccentricity. It isn't. It is an encouragement to gambling in a neighborhood where vice of any kind needs no extra push or sanction from the clergy to flourish. And I'll tell you something else. As a priest, I resent the way Father Britt unloads all the wearisome details of the parish on my shoulders. I'm aware that it's a good thing for me personally at this point in my life to be given the opportunity of acquainting myself with them but as a priest I resent the fact that he plays the lovable eccentric while he palms off the hard work on me. I don't know why I'm telling you all this."

"Because I asked you."

"You asked me. And telling you out loud is not more of a sin than thinking it inside. Does that answer your question?"

"Not quite."

"I'm sure that in later years I'll look back on him as lovable old Father Britt. He'll become a character in my mind. I'll have acquired a little more understanding and compassion . . . or perhaps I'll just be an older priest who is a little more secure and who can afford to think kindly of him because of my own security. Who brought the whisky into the rectory? You, Mr. Gross?"

"Not me, Father," said Mr. Gross. "I rarely drink and then only in moderation."

"I did," said Herman Wekstein. "And it's not whisky, it's bourbon."

"You were going to give me an explanation, Mr. Wekstein."

"Yes, I was. Mr. Gross, do you want to?"

"I said no. I'm explaining nothing except to Father Britt. And I'll deny it to anyone else."

"Mr. Gross manufactures religious articles. Prayer books and statuary . . ."

"I saw that from his card," said Father Kincaid.

"Not really statuary," said Mr. Gross. "Those little figures of saints you see on the dashboards of cars. Perhaps you've seen them, Father? If not I'd be happy to send you one . . ."

"He also," continued Herman, "manufactures religious pictures. Lithographs. One particular picture. A picture of Christ. I think you've seen it."

"Father Britt's crying picture?"

"Father Britt's miracle," said Herman.

"Will you stop calling it a miracle?" asked Dan Gross.

Herman Wekstein told, in detail, about Mr. Gross and his imperfect pictures.

"The bishop suggested something like this was the explanation," said Father Kincaid when he'd finished. "Father Britt will be very embarrassed when he hears about it."

"Embarrassed? Where is your understanding, Father

205

Kincaid? Where is your compassion? Where is your common human sympathy? Embarrassed?"

"He made an honest mistake. He'll be the first to admit it. I think we owe Mr. Gross a debt of gratitude for telling us before we angered the bishop even more."

"Is that all you think about? Angering the bishop? Father Britt *believes* in his miracle."

"But it is no miracle, Mr. Wekstein. I never thought it was."

"I don't give a *damn* what *you* thought. All I care about is Maurie Britt. The man. Maurie Britt. Not Father Britt, your pastor who jumped to the wrong conclusion and will be embarrassed about it."

Herman Wekstein went to the table and poured himself a drink. He looked at the others. Dan Gross started toward him for his glass, looked at Father Kincaid who was shaking his head furiously and stopped and shook *his* head. Herman took a swallow and put the glass back on the table.

When he spoke again, he spoke quietly. There was no anger in his voice. "Father Kincaid, what is your first name?"

Father Kincaid puffed on his pipe. "Everett," he said.

"Call me Herman, will you please? I can't talk to you now as Father Kincaid or have you call me Mr. Wekstein. For God's sake call me Herman."

Father Kincaid nodded his head.

"Listen to me, Everett. Listen to me with your heart. This is an old man who has served your Church. Think of him that way for a moment. More than just served it . . . it was his whole life. You are just starting on what

I think your Church calls a Vocation. Father Britt is coming to the end of his. Are you so sure of yourself and your Call . . . your Vocation . . . that you can have no understanding of a man who has spent his whole life questioning? Not questioning his God . . . questioning himself and his worthiness. It may come as a surprise to you that a man can spend fifty years serving God and still question his worthiness to do so. Does that surprise you?"

"No," said Father Kincaid, "I can understand that."

"I'm not interested in whether this is the true faith . . . whether yours is the true God . . . whether this church of yours deserves the kind of sacrifices it demands of its priests. I *am* interested in Maurie Britt. And I know that he searched his soul every morning of his life. I know that he never felt he was worthy of the miracle of the Mass. You see I've even learned the jargon from him. This is a good man and something happened. Something that we all understand now. It's not hindsight to say that we all suspected that there was the kind of explanation Mr. Gross gave us tonight. All of us except Maurie Britt. To Maurie Britt this was the answer he'd been searching for those fifty years. This was God telling him something very personal and very important. This was his miracle. He *had* to believe in it. And tomorrow morning when Mr. Gross calls him and tells him what he has told us . . . that miracle will have been destroyed and Maurie Britt will be a Catholic priest still searching for assurance and confirmation. Do you have the right to deny him that solace? Do either of you have the right to withhold that assurance from a man who has earned compassion on his knees worshiping your God?"

"It's the truth, Herman. We don't have the right to withhold the truth . . . any of us. You've read the papers. You know what's happening. The Church cannot allow this circus to go on," said Father Kincaid. "Everybody with one of Mr. Gross's imperfect pictures thinks he's been singled out for sainthood. Isn't there an obligation there too?"

"How long can it go on?" asked Herman. "In a few days, Mr. Gross will have repossessed all the pictures in that shipment. With no more crying pictures the whole thing will die out. And what harm's been done? The Church has been in the news . . . St. Martin's has attracted people who have never been inside a church before. And you won't break an old man's heart. Or his spirit. Or, perhaps . . . even his faith."

"Don't sentimentalize. If he is to be reassured that reassurance will come."

"*If* he is to be reassured? If? Forgive me, Everett, if I misquote, but doesn't it say somewhere, "The Lord works in wondrous ways his miracles to perform"? Who's to say this isn't exactly what Father Britt thinks it is? Who's to say, even with Mr. Gross's explanation, that there is not some divine purpose to those pictures crying now? He said it's been happening over the course of almost twenty years. How many can that have been in any given month . . . since he has redeemed some fifteen hundred of them? A couple? Two or three . . . or five? There have been something like thirty or thirty-five of them in two days. Why in only two days? Why that many suddenly?"

"I told you," said Mr. Gross. "It happens all the time. People never thought anything of it except that they got

208

gypped . . . until it hit the newspapers."

"But that many?" asked Herman. "Isn't that an unusually odd number in just a couple of days?"

"I don't think that's the point, Herman," said Father Kincaid. "The point is that you can't suppress the truth. Even to save Father Britt's vanity."

"I'm not trying to save his vanity. I'm trying to save his soul. Listen to me, Everett . . . go along with me for a while. You too, Mr. Gross. Tell the bishop if you must, but only with the understanding that he won't tell Father Britt."

"Tell the bishop?" shouted Mr. Gross. "Are you crazy? I *know* the bishop. I don't tell the bishop and if anyone else tells him I deny it."

"All I'm asking, Everett," said Herman, quietly, "is a little time. I'm asking both of you to say nothing about it now. Just a little time. A little time . . . for sweet charity's sake."

"No, Herman."

Herman sat down and put his head in his hands again. His body started to shake and when he removed his hands the tears rolled down his face and his body shook with sobs.

"For God's sake," he said. "For God's sake. He's a dying man."

"Does he know that?" asked Father Kincaid.

"No. The doctor told me he'll be dead in a matter of a month . . . maybe less. Everett, listen to me. Are you so secure in your own mind that you haven't the slightest doubt that it was meant to be this way? Father Britt's miracle. It lasted just long enough for him to die with a clear conscience, peace of mind, and the assurance that he needs. After that, shout it from the rooftops. Tell the truth."

"I'll deny everything," said Mr. Gross.

"Don't you see? It *is* his miracle. The fact that it is no miracle at all makes it an even greater miracle. It is a miracle to *him*. And it has to remain one until after he's dead."

There was silence in the room.

"Well?" asked Herman.

"I'll do whatever the Father says," said Mr. Gross.

"I guess that puts it up to you, Everett," said Herman Wekstein.

They both looked at the young priest.

"It isn't fair, Herman."

"You're a priest, Everett. That's your Vocation. That's your Call. You know everything there is to know about it now. It's up to you. Not only to Father Kincaid, the priest. To Everett Kincaid, the man, too. You haven't learned to be both yet. He did, Everett. Well?"

"I'd like to pray."

"Do you want us to leave?" asked Herman.

"No. I think I'd like to go to the church . . . to the altar. I'd like to think about Father Britt's miracle there."

Father Kincaid put his pipe on the table and left the room.

"I'm sorry, Mr. Gross," said Herman, "about that violence. I'm not a violent man usually."

"Don't worry about it."

Dan Gross picked up his coat and hat from the chair and carefully folded the coat over his arm. He extended his hand and Herman shook it.

"Don't worry, Mr. Wekstein. I'll wait until Father Kincaid calls me in the morning to tell me what he's decided.

210

I think it has to be his decision now, don't you?"

"Yes. I guess it is his decision."

"Don't bother showing me out. Good-night. I'm sorry I didn't meet Father Britt."

"I'm not. Good-night, Mr. Gross."

Herman Wekstein stood in the empty room for a minute looking around at the furnishings. His eyes rested on the faded wallpaper and the clean, bright space where the picture had hung.

A miracle . . . he thought. Who's to say what's a miracle?

He picked up the bottle of bourbon and carried it out of the room with him. He started out the door. As he reached for the knob he paused. He turned and climbed the stairs to the second floor. At the door to Father Britt's room he paused and listened for a moment. He heard nothing and so he pushed the door open and walked in. He stood over the bed looking down at the old priest.

"Hello, Herman," said Father Britt, quietly.

"Hello, Maurie."

"Still worried about me?"

"I was just thinking how terrible it is to have lived as long as you have and to be just discovering the horror of a hang-over."

"I'm all right, Herman."

"Of course you are."

"No, I mean really all right." The priest smiled.

"I've been thinking Herman. About the pictures. My own personal miracle. I don't think it matters whether they are that or not Herman. At best they're minor miracles. And the world is full of minor miracles. Every spring is

211

a minor miracle. The flowers grow . . . the rain falls, the earth is fertile again. Nobody pays any attention to them. We take these minor, regular miracles for granted. But they are miracles despite that.

"Well the pictures just happened. They are no more or no less important than the other millions of minor miracles around us all the time . . . telling us there is a purpose and a continuity to life. And I suppose Herman I've been thinking about faith. Faith, Herman. Not proof or certainty. Faith. And I think it comes down to something very simple. You can't demand proof. You have to accept. You have to decide between having faith . . . and not having faith. It's that simple. And I suppose Herman . . . it is this simple too. I have faith. With all the doubts and yearning for proof . . . I have faith. It *is* enough Herman. It is enough."

"You know something Maurie," said Herman, "I think you're still trying to convert me."

"I think perhaps I have finally converted myself."

Herman Wekstein closed the door of the priest's bedroom as he left. On the way out he met Mrs. Doody coming up the steps.

Father Maurice Britt died during the night. Mrs. Doody discovered the body when she went to his room to awaken him. The bishop celebrated a solemn Requiem Mass at St. Martin's in his memory. Father Everett Kincaid delivered the eulogy.

There were no more reports of crying pictures.

Ever.

212